STEINOPOLY

JORDAN HILLIGENN

Steinopoly

Published by Kabeeg Publishing (Pty) Ltd

Edenvale, South Africa

www.jordanhilligenn.com

contact@jordanhilligenn.com

ISBN 978-0-620-83791-0

eISBN 978-0-620-83774-3

Layout by Boutique Books

Printed in South Africa by Digital Action

DEDICATION

My beautiful wife Nicóle who would not allow me to settle for anything mediocre.

My children Carter and Isabellé for the inspiration that you both have provided me.

My wonderful parents Alan and Chantél for instilling in me a discipline and dedication to pursue that which sets my heart on fire.

CHAPTER ONE

Search and Seizure

Wikus Louw was fast asleep at 3am on Saturday morning, the 9th of December 2017. He lay in a drunken stupor from emptying his whiskey bottle the night before. He woke up to loud knocking and shouting at his front door but struggled to register what was going on. Not seconds later he heard a loud crash as the special operations team bashed the door down to gain entry into his home. Two dozen officers entered the Louw mansion with Detective Mark Sidd at the helm. Having been violently nudged awake by his wife, Wikus Louw ran to the front door in his pyjama's and slippers, with his wife close behind clutching, at her robe.

"What on earth are you doing? Do you have any idea how much that door cost! It was hand crafted and imported, only one of a kind! Who do you think you are, barging in like this?" he argued with the officers.

He wasn't finished yet. "I'll have my lawyer on all of you for this!"

Before he could utter another threat, Detective Sidd held out a warrant for the search and seizure of anything related to Hillstrong Holdings or business acquisitions in Wikus Louw's personal capacity or related party companies or trusts. The warrant allowed a search of the entire premises and the confiscation of any and all items – whether paper, electronic, storage facility, physical items or anything else at the discretion of the detective in charge – that might serve as evidence before a court of law for the allegations of irregular accounting practices, fraud and illegal dealings in connection with Hillstrong Holdings. In summary, the warrant gave Detective Sidd and his team all powers necessary for a comprehensive search and seizure of anything at the Louw mansion.

Wikus Louw was fuming. He grabbed the warrant and looked at it as if he were going to instantly find a loophole, but then thought better of it and immediately called his lawyer.

Detective Sidd instructed his team to commence with the search and seizure. "You have all been briefed on what we are looking for. If you have any questions, call me immediately. Based on the size of this house, it is going to take a couple of hours. Don't break anything. I am not in the mood to fill in any extra paperwork. You may get started!"

Six teams of four people set to work in different directions. Detective Sidd had procured a blueprint of the house that illustrated the different rooms he had allocated to his teams of men and woman to operate in. It wasn't twenty minutes when an elderly man with greying hair entered the Louw mansion through where the front door used to be. He was dressed in a lawyer's suit and holding a briefcase. He walked inside quickly and looked around for two people: Detective Sidd, being the man in charge, and his boss, who had impressed urgency on him getting there. He stood there out of breath. It seemed like he might have run there out of desperation to avoid disappointing the man who paid his fees.

"I am Hendrik van der Merwe, Mr Louw's legal representative. People call me 'H'. You are, I assume, Detective Mark Sidd?" The detective nodded and shook hands with the old man. "I would like to have a copy of the warrant for my perusal. Let me warn you, one step outside of the authority of the four corners of that document and I will hold you and your team personally liable for any damages or reckless exposure of the business affairs of Mr Louw. Do I make myself clear, Detective Sidd?"

Again the detective nodded and watched the lawyer scurry off to find his employer. Detective Sidd had been more than expecting that encounter. In fact, he had been counting on it.

Detective Sidd stood silently for a moment in his dark blue parker jacket with the words DETECTIVE printed in white and bold on the back. He stroked his moustache with his forefinger and thumb and admired the house. He started walking around the Louw mansion. The artwork, ornaments and furniture were valued at a few hundred million Rand alone. Original parquet flooring and Persian rugs covered the floor throughout. Every room contained either couches or high-backed chairs, with antique and expensive-looking side-tables to match. Crystal chandeliers hung in the entrance hall from a ceiling at the top of a double story wooden staircase.

He knew where he was most interested in looking – the home office – and found it after ten minutes of walking around and getting lost due to the number of passages, the size of the house and the distraction of all of its contents. The home office itself was about the size of half of the detective's entire house. Bookshelves with books and memorabilia covered two walls, and there were more Persian rugs, two fire places and dark brown leather couches. He could only imagine that this was where Wikus Louw and his associates sat and drank whiskey and smoked cigars while discussing the various multi-billion Rand deals he was so famously known for. The room had a view through four large floor-to-ceiling glass doors that led out to a balcony.

At the far end of the room was a massive desk where the man himself would sit. Detective Sidd remembered reading in a magazine article that the imported desk was made from six different types of wood, including ebony and elm, with a glass top to finish it off, and was valued at over two hundred thousand dollars.

The rest of the office was much the same: paintings on the walls valued at millions of dollars or pounds, depending on their origin. The theme of the office was a mixture of wealth and Afrikaans heritage. Next to an old hunting rifle on the wall hung a magnificent oil on canvas painting of a man dressed in French attire, rearing a horse and pointing upwards, titled "Napoleon Crossing the Alps" and dated 1801. Surrounding the artwork were various photographs of Wikus and his friends at luxurious wine estates and many of him shaking hands with other famous people, leaders of countries, and other worldwide billionaires. These photographs hung above shelves of glass trophies for the various merger and acquisition transactions that he concluded for Hillstrong Holdings.

Detective Sidd approached the desk and sat in the high-back leather chair. He had never felt such comfort. If his office had a chair like this he would retire from investigations and be more than happy with a desk job. On the desk was a state-of-the-art office phone, a laptop, a desk calendar with writing on certain dates as reminders for meetings.

The previous month's calendar had been ripped off unevenly and there was an impression on the current month's page from a previous month's entry. He couldn't read it all, but it seemed to be a conference call with someone whose initials were "FH". He would get his team to send that to the lab. He could take a pencil and lightly rub over it and the writing would appear easier to read, but decided to leave it to the experts.

Also on the glass-topped wooden desk were three gold ornaments. Two formed a set illustrating a bull and a bear, the symbols representing different views of the stock market. The third was a golden fish of some sort, about the size of a coffee mug and rendered in incredible detail. He was fascinated by the scales and level of detail. The golden fish was attached to a red velvet base with a small plaque that read "Become the Dragon". He picked it up; it was as heavy as one would think a chunk of solid gold would weigh. If it wasn't solid gold, it must be damn close to being so.

He went through the drawers briefly, but nothing was out of the ordinary. He leaned back in the chair and swiveled around looking at the bookcases behind the desk and the various books and ornaments that lay upon the shelves. He was admiring the detail of the wood again when something caught his eye. If he hadn't been in that exact position he might have missed it. There was a strand of material that the light above the desk had caught, squashed between the bookshelves. He ran his fingers over the wood – it was perfectly smooth. It would be highly unlikely that any piece of clothing would catch and leave behind a thread, or even fluff, unless the shelves were either damaged or… if they were moved apart. He looked around for any sort of handle or button that could prove him right. He called one of his team members to come to the office with the blueprints of the house. According to the house plans, there shouldn't be anything behind this bookcase besides a brick wall.

He was hoping to find something incriminating behind this bookshelf. As the bookshelves were floor to ceiling and covered the entire back wall of the office, it was impossible to look behind them. Was the piece of material sufficient to justify taking these expensive shelves apart? Was his hunch worth the risk of being held personally liable for damage to these exquisite wood features? He didn't want to imagine what they had cost.

"Call Mr Louw here, please," he instructed a member of his team.

A few minutes later Wikus Louw and his lawyer entered the office. "Mr Louw, is there anything behind this bookshelf?" the detective asked.

It was not Wikus Louw who answered but his lawyer. "I have instructed my client not to answer any questions unless subpoenaed by the courts to do so."

Hardly surprising. Detective Sidd watched Wikus Louw's expression, hoping for any sign of fear that they might be on to something, but there was no hint on the face of this professional businessman who bluffed and negotiated billion-Rand deals on a daily basis. It was also difficult to judge any expression on the hungover man's face. "Very well, Mr Louw, you may leave."

Wikus Louw and his lawyer turned to leave the office when Detective Sidd noticed a split second glance that Wikus gave to his desk. Did that mean anything? What was he looking at? The ornaments, the calendar, possibly the computer? Well, he guessed he would have to confiscate everything then. Detective Sidd spent another futile half hour looking around the shelves for any hint on how to move them. Nothing was forthcoming.

A team, along with a forensic photographer, entered the office and the photographer took more than one photograph of every single item in the room and of the room as a whole. The team proceeded to search and package all items, paperwork, the laptop, even the office phone. One of his team members told him that certain new phone models, like the one on Wikus Louw's desk, contained a storage facility or function to record phone calls. If the owner of the phone did not wish to update the recording to a cloud drive, then the model included a micro SD card that would store all the recordings. This model included one, which the forensic personnel removed and placed in a small paper bag.

The team left the office to continue with the rest of the many rooms of the mansion. Detective Sidd could not bring himself to leave the room yet. He once again felt all around the desk and the bookshelves. The room was much emptier after all the items were removed and packaged; there was no secret book lever that opened the door, no ornament attached to the shelf as a handle, like one would see in the movies. If there was something, it had to be some form of button, maybe something even more subtle. As he was pressing on the front side of the bookshelf, at around shoulder height, he heard a faint "click" sound. Just as he'd thought: a pressure switch that would only work if deliberately pressed.

The heavy bookshelf eased its way towards the detective, exposing a walk-in safe. The bookshelf was attached to the safe door. On the metal shelves inside the safe were files of paperwork, stacks of money bound by rubber bands, jewelry, as well as memory cards in specialised cases. He stood back in amazement. He had hit the jackpot.

He again consulted the blueprints of the house to see if there was anything he'd missed. No, the plans were created deliberately to mislead anyone reading them that this walk-in safe existed. He called the team back, along with Wikus Louw and his lawyer.

"Mr Louw, we have found your walk-in safe. My team here is going to photograph everything in your presence and itemise all of the safe's contents. Thereafter, we are going to package everything and remove it offsite for examination. As the content of this safe appears to be of high value, you will be required to sign off on the itemised document before leaving. I will leave the team and yourself to conclude this process."

Wikus Louw and his lawyer were speechless and looked very pale. The defeated Wikus Louw nodded and sat down on his leather couch while the special ops personnel unpacked the safe item by item and wrote down a description of each item on the list.

Detective Sidd was satisfied with his find. You can't beat old school detective hunches, he thought. The rest of the mansion was searched. The items seized would probably be worthless to their case in comparison to that safe and Wikus Louw's office, but they would in any event take everything for investigation. It was now 6AM. He would wait another hour before alerting the public prosecutor, Rhonda Martins, of the events of the morning. For now he would go get himself a hot breakfast and a coffee. He had, after all, earned it.

CHAPTER TWO

Court

NEWS BROADCASTERS ACROSS THE GLOBE were covering the same story that had gone viral:

International retail giant, Hillstrong Holdings, admitted it is unable to release financial statements due to accounting irregularities, confirming recent market rumours about the furniture retailer.

The statement has sent shock-waves through international stock markets, causing the share price of Hillstrong Holdings to drop more than 5% in a matter of hours. The price continues to drop as investors fear for the loss of their life savings. Banks have instituted urgent legal proceedings to prevent any drastic disposals by the conglomerate, while loans worth billions of Rands may be defaulted upon because of the drop in the share price. Many lenders have accepted Hillstrong shares as security for loans.

This is undoubtedly heading towards being South Africa's largest corporate crash in history. Economic and market commentators have compared this event to the US Enron scandal.

This news, along with the resignation of the Chief Executive Officer, Wikus Louw, led to a joint overnight search and seizure operation, headed by the Public Prosecutor's Office and the Commercial Crimes Division. The offices of Hillstrong Holdings as well as the home of Wikus Louw were raided by a special operations team in the early hours of this morning. Will the executives be held accountable? Investigations are underway. Be sure to stay tuned for the unfolding of this breaking news on CNN News.

Millions of South Africans watched the broadcast while similar broadcasts were viewed all over the world in different languages. The same symbols, graphs and share codes were being shown by all broadcasters – but viewers did not need to understand the language to know what the story was about.

***

Josh Carter raced his Ducati Panigale V4 motorcycle through the streets of Johannesburg. It was early on Sunday morning. The roads were quiet and the air fresh, allowing him to experience the freedom he so often craved and forget about all the stresses of life. It made him forget all about the long week – a long couple of weeks – preparing for trial and performing for the judge.

He wasn't particularly optimistic about his latest case. His client's witnesses had crumbled under cross examination. They were inconsistent and what they'd orally testified to had come across as contradictory to the written witness statements that were disclosed with the pleadings. He did not necessarily think of the witnesses as dishonest at all. Quite the opposite. It was just the pressure of being in the witness box and the way the opposing counsel would twist statements in an attempt to paint the witness in a bad light. Nerves made people run their mouths off; it was the nerves speaking most of the time.

A witness was often asked a yes or no question and they would end up telling the court what they had for breakfast, something completely irrelevant to the question. Often that portrayed what was called a "good witness". It was the witnesses who were too calm and delivered their testimony too well who were "bad witnesses". These witnesses had rehearsed too well, or were possibly coached by the questioning lawyer. However, once Josh had given his closing argument he felt the odds were slightly improved but still not more in his favour than that of his opponent, although he couldn't really tell until the judge took a decision. The decision was to be handed down the next morning at 10AM before Justice Naidoo.

The Ducati's engine roared as Josh held the accelerator open and climbed through the gears – the bike was powerful and agile. The unmistakable Ducati-red bike flew past the other bike enthusiasts who were also on the road, not because Josh's bike was that much faster than the rest – it wasn't – but because Josh had nerves of steel and a competitive streak that would not see him let up on the throttle before any opponent. Opponent, as if every other bike rider on the road was competing against him.

The road was quiet. The acceleration of the Ducati increased from 0-100km/h in just a few seconds, pumping adrenaline through Josh's veins with every twist of his wrist opening the throttle... 100km/h... holding the throttle open, 160km/h feeling the wind against his body getting stronger and the scream of the engine getting louder. At 210km/h it was just him and his bike. He was still holding the throttle open, redlining each gear, lifting his left foot to shift into the next gear; 260km/h... the road was getting shorter and so he was forced to slow down as he reached a T-junction. After looking left and right, he drove away from the city, out to the roads that took him past the farmlands.

It was amazing how quickly a person left the Johannesburg skyscrapers behind and was surrounded by beautiful open lands. Working and living in the city, it felt like the buildings and man-made structures carried on forever. Every day was so planned-out and structured. So, he allowed himself this joy every once in a while. To not plan the route of his bike ride, to explore new areas and roads and find his way back home.

Returning home, as he approached his street corner he accelerated as much as possible with his Ducati at peak revs so that his bike could be heard by his neighbours. He was doing this specifically for one neighbour, maybe two. His house, which was situated towards the end of the street in a cul de sac, approached quickly.

Just as he had expected, ahead of him a boy, aged seven, ran out of the front door of his home to watch Josh arrive. His mother was not far behind, reprimanding her son, telling him that he can't just run out into the street without her. Daniel paid almost no notice to his mother, who now held him against her as he jumped up and down waving at Josh. Gabriela also waved at Josh. Josh lifted his visor, revealing his light blue eyes, and returned a wave to the two as he pulled into his driveway. He couldn't help but notice how beautiful Gabby looked, as usual.

Josh often wondered how she kept it all together, being a single mother, divorced from a pathetic excuse of a man who didn't appreciate what he'd had. Gabby had said her ex was more interested in booze and other women than being a father and husband. She wasn't the type of person to wait around for that. She was a real estate agent and interior designer and did well for herself and Daniel.

Josh and Gabby had been friends for about three years now, ever since she and Daniel moved in across the road and she'd come over to introduce herself. Josh ended up assisting her with her divorce proceedings and they spent more and more time together after that and for the last couple of months were now seeing each other on a more intimate level. They kept things extremely casual and there was definitely no label to define them, whatever "them" meant. Neither of them wanted to upset the status quo, though Josh knew that often-times this was exactly what caused so much confusion between couples.

When exactly do you become a couple? When you tell at least one person that you're a couple, he guessed. In any event, the way things were allowed him to concentrate on his work and also have someone in his life. He often looked after Daniel when she had to show a house early morning on the weekend. Gabby would walk Daniel across the road to visit with Josh and Daniel would usually spend his time looking at Josh's Ducati in the garage or playing the PlayStation that Josh had no more time for. Owning his own law firm gave Josh the freedom to work his own hours, which usually meant working longer hours than usual, including some weekend work.

Josh parked the Ducati in the double extra-wide garage next to his recently purchased white BMW M4 hardtop convertible. He hung his leather jacket and helmet in his garage cupboard. His short blonde hair had been squashed into "helmet hair" by the helmet. Josh generally kept his hair neat and trimmed because of the bike riding. He wore a t-shirt that fit his well-built athletic frame.

As a bachelor, he lived in a very modern home, but it did have a few feminine touches thanks to Gabby who, over time, had kindly offered her interior design expertise to "liven up" his home; make it "less boring", she had said. She'd made the comments one day after fetching Daniel. It hadn't taken her long until she was comfortable enough to speak her mind with Josh. Josh liked that she was a straight shooter. She'd felt it might be nice to add a woman's touch to his home, even if it were without a woman for the time being.

Josh pressed the chrome button, selecting a cappuccino on his sleek black Jura coffee machine, popped two slices of bread in the toaster and sat at his kitchen table with his laptop open on the news. The Hillstrong Holdings scandal dominated all headlines. He hadn't read much of the news lately – he never did when preparing for a trial, when he submerged himself in all the paperwork. He had to know the facts and details better than the opposing lawyer. Besides, the news these days just depressed him. He did a quick scan of the main story that was still breaking and did not contain many facts yet. Journalists had, however, already managed to take photographs of the ex-CEO's home and cars in the driveway, really portraying him as a grossly rich man caught enjoying his wealth while the country experienced the worst financial loss of pensions and retirement funds in history.

Josh moved on to the sports news. He was a motor racing fan, naturally. There would be the Formula One race broadcast from Qatar later that evening. He found out which teams the front grid would be comprised of and smiled at the result that his favourite two teams were in the top two rows – Ferrari and Red Bull. There was pop sound; his toast was ready. Nothing further interested him on the news.

He buttered and jammed his toast and made his way outside to the pool to enjoy his breakfast. It was a beautiful morning. He lounged on his deck chairs next to his miniature Japanese garden – his pride and joy that had taken many months to complete. Stones, sand, a little stream that flowed into a small koi pond with an over-arching bridge. A small school of koi swam in the pond. Just enough to avoid overcrowding the pond. Each fish was carefully chosen for its different colours and stories behind the patterns and marks on their scales. His garden could easily be featured in a magazine. Josh spent his down-time here; it was therapeutic.

He had taken an interest in the Japanese and Chinese culture after being advised by a doctor to practice meditation to alleviate the stress he experienced in his career. He had a habit of becoming too obsessive and competitive and was warned that if he was not able to find a healthy and more balanced lifestyle he would be prone to heart attacks in his forties already.

It was a perfect day to catch up on all the things he would usually do routinely now that his trial work was completed. He usually spent his weekends on bike riding, exercising, car washing and shopping for groceries, but this trial had asked a lot more of him than usual and so he had been skipping this routine for the last few weeks. The stakes of his trial were higher, the paperwork thicker, and the facts more complicated. It also didn't help his stress levels that the trial attracted media coverage – something he wasn't quite used to.

It hadn't helped matters that the media did not always portray their persons of interest in the best light: that wouldn't make for interesting news. Josh was also known as a lawyer with a temper. Often in the court room he would be asked by the judge to stop shouting or not to be too aggressive towards his opponents. He became really popular when one of the opposing lawyers had got up in his face to provoke him and he'd attempted to push the lawyer away from him but, with the scuffle and everyone around them, it accidentally turned into a slap in the face. Josh had tried to explain himself but ended up paying a fine in court.

He got dressed to go to the gym and go grocery shopping thereafter, to break the bad habit of eating the fast foods he had been living on all week. He climbed into his BMW, inhaled the new car smell and the scent of the leather seats, and exhaled slowly. The smell was addictive, just like the smell of racing fuel. He pushed the engine start button and the 3.2 litre MTwinPower Turbo in-line 6-cylinder petrol engine growled to life. The garage door hummed open and he reversed out onto his driveway. Gabby and Daniel were on their way out too. He gave Gabby a smile and waved to Daniel for the second time that morning.

Gabby rolled down her car window. "Hello. You've been out and about today," she said.

"My trial is finally over after five weeks of hell, so I finally get to have a life for a bit," Josh answered. Gabby knew about the trial, how could she not? Even if Josh didn't discuss the cases he worked on, the trial was all over the news. During the first few weeks when it hit the media there had been TV crews parked outside Josh's house, trying to interview him and get any comments that he was willing to share. They'd even tried to interview her once or twice but she was very insistent that she would not speak to them about her "neighbour", as she referred to him. If the media got any wind that they might be more than friends it would just offer opportunities for the gossip columns.

"I heard on the news yesterday that it had finished and that all that is left is for the Judge to make a ruling. When will you find out how it went?" she asked.

"Tomorrow, so hold thumbs." He gestured holding thumbs to her and winked at Daniel. Daniel could not take his eyes off of Josh's new BMW.

Josh asked, "Do you like my new wheels?"

"It's just like the model in the PlayStation game!" he exclaimed.

"That's right, bud! How about I take you for a spin later today?" Josh offered. Daniel nodded in excitement.

"You know that he is going to sit and wait for you the entire day now," Gabby said with a smile.

"I know. I was the same at his age, and when I get into this new car I feel like I am still his age," Josh grinned. "I'm going to get some exercise and re-stock my fridge with better food than take-outs. I'll be watching the F1 Grand Prix later today, if Daniel wants to join me. I'll give him a ride around the block just before and we can make home-made tortillas, if you're interested?" Josh wondered if that sounded a bit desperate.

"I'm sure he would love that. I wouldn't mind seeing you either. See you later."

Josh waved goodbye and with his seven-year-old self in his white BMW roared the engine to life and sped off, leaving black tyre tracks up the road.

The gym was near empty, just the way Josh liked it. He jogged a few kilometres on the treadmill and then made his way to the weights section. He prided himself on his fitness and strength. He trained like a navy seal with extreme cardio and heavy lifting.

"Josh, how are you doing, bud?" It was a former colleague of Josh's, Dave. They'd remained in contact ever since Josh had left the world of Big Law and opened up his own firm.

"Dave, good to see you. I'm well. How are things at the firm?"

"It's cut-throat, to be honest. Everyone is fighting for clients; new business just isn't coming in. Fortunately, I have a few long-standing clients so my job is safe for now. I often think about following in your footsteps and going out on my own but just don't feel brave enough for that yet. The firm offers clients comfort that a small firm can't always provide in the beginning. We all follow your latest trials. There was talk that the head of department was retiring and your name was mentioned to come back in. Do you think you would be interested in Big Law again?" Dave asked in a way that sounded as if he was concerned that Josh would swoop in take his own job from him.

"I'll never go back. I enjoy working my own cases, hours and not answering to anybody else, except for the client of course," said Josh.

"I thought so," Dave said, sounding relieved. "What do you make of the latest corporate scandal with Hillstrong Holdings? What a shit show. The firm is desperately trying to bring in more clients as a result of the losses. Problem is, it would have to be on a contingency basis because any client would have lost a lot of money and would not be able to pay the fees unless their claims are successful."

"There's not only that. When an international corporation goes belly up after such a severe scandal, it's highly unlikely that the share price will recover enough to recoup the losses. If you look at the size of Hillstrong's market share and the decrease in share price, we're talking about losses in the billions and at least double digits. It's catastrophic," said Josh.

Dave didn't seem to have thought too much about the complexities of the matter. "Shit, you're right, Josh. Anyway, I'd better be going now. I have to go into the office to finish a brief. See you around!"

"Cheers, Dave. Good luck! Send my regards to the guys at the firm!" said Josh.

"Will do!" shouted Dave as he left the weight room.

Bench-press and bicep curls were Josh's favourite exercises. He loved how the adrenalin pump and strength increase made him feel. Physical exercise was something where you could see results, especially strength gain.

His father was a massive powerlifter back in the day. He would always say that an average man in the street wouldn't even be able to bench press his own body weight. After hearing that as a youngster, Josh made sure that he could always bench press an impressive amount.

Every young boy likes to think that their dad is the biggest and strongest, but while growing up Josh knew this to be the truth about his. Alan Carter was six foot three and weighed 135 kilograms in his prime. His wife, Josh's mother Elizabeth, had to cut the sleeves off his t-shirts so that they would fit him. In his home town, Springs, in the far East Rand, Alan often made the newspapers with his powerlifting competitions and weight training. He would start gym at 4AM and go to work at 6:30AM and complete a second session from 7PM to 9PM at least five times a week. He would regularly eat whole chickens and dozens of eggs. He had a handshake that could bring a grown man to tears.

Josh had also developed his passion for speed and engines from his father. It was something they shared and bonded over. He made a mental note to phone his parents later to check in.

After an hour of exercise Josh was feeling on top of the world. His kitchen cupboards were full; he had bought some snacks and drinks for the F1 Grand Prix later. It was about lunch time and he could relax and do some light leisure reading, maybe even take a nap.

His phone buzzed with an email from a client requesting an amendment to a business agreement. Could Josh get him a first draft in the next day or two? Yes he could, and he would. No nap for him. Josh preferred it this way. He had to stay productive, always moving forward. He found it difficult to relax if he thought there was something he could be doing to either progress his professional life or improve his learning. Owning his own law firm also meant he had to make sure he brought the business in every month. He would only start the drafting the next day, but would at least read the current agreement again to refresh his memory.

Just before sunset Josh looked out into the street where Daniel was riding his bicycle while Gabby watched him and shouted to him to be careful. Living in a cul de sac meant the street was relatively quiet and Daniel could ride his bicycle up and down without having to watch out for traffic. Josh went outside through the garage. He barely made it halfway across the street on his way to Gabby before Daniel noticed him and threw his bicycle down onto the grass and ran to him, asking if he was going to take him for a ride in the new car.

"You have created a monster," Gabby laughed.

"Yes, bud. That's if you're still up for it?" Of course Daniel would be up for it. Gabby seemed very impressed with the car too. While driving he sneaked a few glances at her smiling in the passenger seat. She did the same to him. Daniel, in the back, was grinning ear to ear. He vowed that when he grew older he would be a lawyer just like Josh and also own bikes and cars.

They returned home. Josh put on the racing and poured himself and Gabby a drink. Daniel went and sat in his favourite spot on the corner of the couch and remained glued to the TV for the duration of the race, asking a question every now and then about the racing procedures. Josh and Gabby stood in the kitchen watching Daniel while discussing work and life. They spoke about dinner plans that had fallen through due to both their busy schedules. Having no babysitter for Daniel did not make matters any easier when it came to making adult plans.

Daniel watched almost the entire race before falling asleep sometime during the last ten laps. He would be happy to hear that his favourite drivers, who were also Josh's favourite drivers, had placed first and third. Josh picked Daniel up and carried him across the road while talking softly to Gabby. "Thank you for making his day with the car and then having us over. It means a lot to him, and to me. He really looks up to you, Josh," Gabby said.

Josh could hear the sincerity in the mother's voice. "No problem. It's great to have him around, and you." He smiled sheepishly. After putting Daniel to bed, Josh kissed Gabby on the cheek and said goodnight. He'd turned to leave when she reached out and touched his arm. He faced her and she stepped up on her toes to kiss him on the mouth. It was quick, but passionate.

"That's how you say goodnight! Why do I have to make the first move?" she said playfully.

"I'll have to work on that!" said Josh, "good night."

"Goodnight, Josh."

What a beautiful night to go for a stroll before retiring to bed before his big day in court tomorrow. A night walk was a great way to clear the head, make sense of all his thoughts about work, his life and, of course, Gabby.

Had Josh not been lost in a day dream he may have noticed the man standing in the shadows, watching him, as he had been for the last few hours.

CHAPTER THREE

Court Decision

MONDAY MORNING WAS A BLUR. Josh was at the court before the hustle and bustle of weekday traffic. His client, John Archer of Archer Resources, was present to hear the judgement personally. It was a very important case for the company and would have serious financial consequences whichever way it went and so the board had asked him to audit the court hearing. Josh had prepared him for the worst; a decision against them would tarnish their reputation and spread through the market like wildfire. He hoped for the best, though. He always did, no matter how badly he felt the case had gone.

Josh had done a great job, considering how difficult his client had made the case for him. He had not been provided with the best evidence to put forward, but ultimately it was his closing argument that brought all the evidence together in such a logical manner that could have sealed the deal for them. They were about to find out.

In walked opposing counsel, a vicious Pitbull of a woman, Veronica Kane. Josh and Veronica had studied together and both had taken up articles in large law firms and then in the same year started their own practices. Veronica had suggested a partnership with Josh but he'd decided to go his own way as a sole practitioner. She'd set up her practice with two other partners.

They greeted each other professionally and briefly; no smart comments or jabs, especially not right before a decision where they could be made to feel foolish in ten minutes' time. In any event, the fights were never personal, strictly business.

She wasn't bad looking at all; she just had a hard look on her face all the time, as if she were on the offensive. She was career obsessed, just like Josh, and seemed to have a grudge against the male species as a whole. Josh could only remember one occasion where she'd let her hair down, literally, and had actually had a smile on her face. He'd had a conversation with her and found her to be quite pleasant underneath that tough exterior. She had an impressive track record, though when weighing up the wins and losses against Josh he was in a class of his own.

They waited for Judge Naidoo to enter. The Registrar asked everyone to rise for the Judge. Judge Naidoo entered, greeted counsel on both sides and directed everyone to be seated. Without wasting any time, the Judge started reading her decision.

"This case was a complex one. I am indebted to both counsel for all their efforts and patience in taking me through the evidence and providing expert opinions."

The case was a commercial dispute regarding transport of valuable products, gold bars to be specific. The product belonging to Archer Resources had gone missing and liability had to be determined. Veronica Kane acted for the transport company which alleged that it was an elaborate plan to defraud the insurance company in the event the transport company was not held liable. The complexity of the case arose due to the transport contract not making provision for the situation the parties now found themselves in. That was stereotypically always the situation in litigation – no clear answer.

On top of that, because the transport company was a global brand and the product being transported had to cross international borders, the contract was subject to foreign law. Going up against a global entity meant they had deep pockets; they had large budgets for their litigation fund. The product had not simply gone missing. The consignment packages had arrived at their destination. What was, however, alleged to have been shipped was entirely different to what was found when opening the packages. The gold bars had been switched out for off-cuts of rusted metal bars. This ensured that the weight of the consignment was consistent throughout the journey of transport and therefore was not flagged at any of the inspection points.

It sounded simple enough, except there were various administrative mistakes on both sides, so the documentary evidence wasn't very conclusive. Video footage from the transport vehicles and destination could, conveniently for the transport company, not be retrieved off a "corrupted" hard drive. The consignment's outer packaging had also been tampered with, but it could not be proven at which stage of the transport leg this occurred.

Then there was the issue of Josh's witnesses giving contradictory evidence. This had allowed Veronica to paint a picture of Josh's client fabricating the whole story as a cover up to sell the product to two parties, making it seem like the packages had been intercepted en-route to the destination.

Judge Naidoo continued with the reading of her decision. "After careful consideration of all the evidence before this court, I have come to the decision that the Claimant, as the Seller of the valuable product, did in fact package the valuable product and that the valuable product did change hands at the premises of the Seller. The Respondent, as the transport company, upon signature of the shipping documents, took over liability for the product at the premises of the Seller. I have not been persuaded by the

Respondent that it performed all duties required of it to ensure that the package was handled responsibly and with due care. It is for this reason that I find for the Claimant and award costs in the Claimant's favour with interest at the legal rate. The written judgement will be sent to the parties by the end of the day. Should the Respondent wish to appeal this judgement, it has thirty days to do so."

Josh's client grabbed him and hugged him and thanked him. Another one in the success column. This would get vast media coverage due to the sum of the judgement awarded being in the millions of Rands, which would in turn refer more cases to him. This was great news. Veronica Kane, clearly not happy with the outcome, simply nodded at Josh before leaving the court room, immediately followed by her client. Josh waited for the court room to empty before leaving. As they watched the court empty, Josh noticed the public prosecutor, Rhonda Martins, leaving the courtroom. What was she doing at the decision of his trial? What interest could she possibly have in this matter?

As it was, she did not have an interest in his matter; she had an interest in him.

They knew what was waiting for them outside – a sea of reporters, cameras and journalists. Josh, not being one to give his comments during the trial, would have to say something now. They were bombarded with microphones, cameras and reporters shouting questions at them. Josh put his hands up to silence the crowd and they immediately fell quiet so as not to miss or misquote anything Josh had to say.

"Today is an example of the law in favour of the truth. The international transport corporation, despite all the money thrown at this case, was on the wrong side of the truth. Obviously, we are very happy with the ruling and with being awarded costs as well. They have thirty days to appeal, so I guess we won't know if it's really over until then. We are of the view that should they proceed with an appeal we will receive the same outcome." Josh answered a few one-on-one questions with the news channel, set up an interview with Lawyers Weekly Magazine for the next day, and left with his client.

The celebratory lunch was at Josh's favourite restaurant, Isabelle's. Despite Josh phoning ahead to book a table, the owner, Vivian Rose, would have made a table available, regardless of how busy she was. Josh knew her personally. Intimately. Vivian greeted and seated Josh and John Archer personally.

"Hey, Vee." Josh greeted Vivian with a peck on the cheek.

"I heard you won. It just hit the midday news. Congratulations, Mr Big Time," she said endearingly.

"Thanks, Vee. Could you bring a bottle of your finest and two orders of the chef's specialty?" he asked.

"You got it, Mr Big Time." She smiled and, brushing his arm with affection, locked down the order with the most experienced waiter.

Vivian Rose had lost her husband in an accident caused by unsafe working conditions at a construction site. He was a good couple of years older than Josh and it was one of the first cases that Josh had tried when he opened up his own practice. Despite Josh needing money, he'd taken on the case on a contingency basis with the risk that if he lost he wouldn't see a cent.

He'd negotiated a large settlement for her that he'd advised she should accept. The company responsible, rather than plead guilty, paid her off to avoid bad press. It had been difficult for Josh to persuade her to accept the deal, but he was certain it was a no-brainer, ensuring she was paid well considering that at the time her husband was the bread winner of the family. It had been five years since her husband had died and nothing would bring him back. She'd used the settlement money to open the restaurant.

Vivian Rose and Josh had a complicated relationship. They cared for each other like mother and son, as she was half a decade older than he, but there was a level of intimacy between them. Over time they had spent many late nights together at Isabelle's when she was supervising the dinner shift and Josh was finishing up work late and needed a bite to eat and, often, a drink. He took all his clients there for lunches and networking and after a hard day in court he went there alone to the bar for a drink, or a few, and a deep chat with her.

John Archer expressed his gratitude for the win with a cheers and a clink of wine glasses. He reached into his navy chequered suit jacket and handed Josh an envelope, emblazoned with the Archer Industries brand.

"What's this?" Josh asked.

"I know that our company has you on retainer, but the board of directors decided that, should you win this case for us, we would pay you a success bonus. A very large one. Considering that we did not make your job any easier with the evidentiary support that you required, and you had to pick up the slack, we figured that you've earned this one!"

"Thanks, John," he said. "I'm grateful for the bonus and the business."

Josh and John Archer enjoyed their meals and wine and parted ways. Vivian Rose was busy at another table when Josh left, so he gave her a wave and a smile that she returned. Josh went back to the office to read some emails and check in with his secretary, Shirley Templeman. She had also left the large firm to follow Josh. They worked well together. She had a large mop of curly blonde-dyed hair and wore pink reading glasses. He had been relieved when she hired on with him; a good legal secretary was hard to find.

Josh Carter and Shirley Templeman were the cogs in the Carter & Associates machine. Perhaps one day Josh would actually hire an associate, but for the time being that would be the team:

a secretary who had been around the block of a law firm, and a damn good lawyer who was becoming a big name.

"Hello, Mr Carter. Congratulations on another win!" Shirley greeted Josh as he walked into the office. She'd called him by his first name at the large firm but, now she'd followed him to his own firm, she insisted it be "Mr Carter". She said it gave him the recognition he had earned and she would ensure he received that from her. She had not worked solely for him at the large firm, as the secretaries generally assisted more than one lawyer, but Josh had been her favourite to work with and she'd made that clear to him.

"Hello, Shirley. Thank you. Any messages for me?" he asked in an "I-enjoyed-my-lunch-a-bit-too-much" voice.

Shirley Templeman followed Josh to his office while giving him the messages. "Only two. Your father phoned to speak to you about his next race at Kyalami racetrack. He wanted to know whether you would like to bring Daniel along again. I said you would be most pleased to accept those tickets and thanked him very much. The second message was from Veronica Kane and she asked that you call her back."

A phone call from opposing counsel shortly after the trial generally meant only one thing – she was calling to inform him that she would be appealing the decision of that morning and if he so much as thought for a second it was over then she would make it clear for him and so on.

"And then there was an unmarked envelope delivered a short while ago. I've placed it in your in-tray."

"Thanks, Shirley." He sat down in his leather chair behind his cherry wood desk and looked out his wall-sized glass windows at the city of Sandton. His own little view in his own firm after a victory. Life was treating him well.

This time he did notice the man wearing a black hat and jacket standing down on the street below, watching him. It was a warm day and so wearing a jacket occurred to Josh as being a bit odd. However, Josh dismissed it, assuming that the man was waiting for an Uber. He checked some emails and opened the envelope he'd received earlier from Archer Industries. The cheque was a very generous success bonus – R100 000 would definitely come in handy.

"I'd better call Veronica back and get it over with and inform the client that there will be more work to do," he thought.

She answered on the second ring. "Veronica Kane."

"Veronica, Josh. I'm returning your call."

"Yes, hi. Just a collegial call to let you know my client will not be appealing the decision."

"Oh, great. Well thanks for the call. I wasn't expecting that."

"I told him I could take you in the next round but apparently your performance was somewhat impressive and the board couldn't justify throwing away another couple of hundred thousand and risk costs as well. You shouldn't have won this matter based on the evidence before the court. You know that, right?"

Josh knew his case had been weak, but what his evidence lacked he'd made up for in his argument and by poking holes in her witnesses during cross-examination.

"It wasn't in my favour, no," he admitted. "Thanks for the call, Veronica. Next time."

"Next time."

The call ended and Josh couldn't think this day could get any better. He looked out of the window again and the man in the black hat and jacket was still there. Just hanging around.

He turned his attention to the blank envelope that Shirley had left for him. His head was still buzzing from the wine, or at least was until he started reading the contents of the letter when he sobered up very quickly. It was a request for a meeting from the Public Prosecutor with a subject line which read "By order of the state this correspondence is confidential and for the intended recipient only". This in itself was not peculiar but the person requesting the meeting certainly was. After reading the contents of the envelope he glanced outside again, but the man had left.

CHAPTER FOUR

Meeting Request

JOSH BEGAN HIS MORNING WITH a run through the quiet streets of Sandton. The sun wasn't up yet, the city not yet awake. Steam rose through the drainage systems, air conditioning vents laboured mechanically, while a lonely vehicle hummed in the distance. He ran up Rivonia Road, past the train station towards the upper-class hotels. He remembered the day when he'd had his first interview in Sandton at a large law firm. He was still in his second year at university in Pretoria. The large firms always recruited their candidates two and even three years before finishing law school. It was the first time he'd travelled by train and also the first time he'd been to Sandton, the richest square mile in Africa. It was the closest he would get to the apartment in New York he'd often told his mother he would live in, without leaving the country.

His interview was only in the afternoon, but he had arrived early in the morning to make sure he knew where he was going. He'd walked around the malls and streets, experiencing the city life that he'd always dreamt about. He'd even had his shoes shined on the curb outside one of the many hotels.

He continued jogging. He turned left on West Street and continued upwards through the high-rise buildings, nodding at Godfrey, the doorman of the Rafael Royale Hotel.

"Top of the morning to ya, Mr Carter," he shouted after Josh.

Running mindlessly without distraction was a great way for Josh to clear his head. It was also a way to think on autopilot. He couldn't get the same effect from riding his motorcycle as that entailed handling the electronics and changing gears. He considered what he would do about the meeting request he'd received the previous afternoon. He had a week to decide whether he would take the meeting, but did not yet know what the case would involve. Naturally, the meeting would lead to a case, but what did Rhonda Martins, Public Prosecutor, want a meeting with him for?

He ran his five-kilometre morning run, ending at the end of his street, and walked the last few hundred metres to his home as a cooling off stint. He reached his driveway and peered across the road to see if there was any life at Gabby's place. He could see a light on in the kitchen; she was obviously fixing Daniel some breakfast. He decided to have an early morning at the office rather than work from home.

He just missed the traffic on his way in to Carter & Associates. He sat down in his comfortable leather chair and asked Shirley to make him some coffee.

"Your coffee, Mr Carter," she said as she placed it down on his desk.

"Thanks, Shirley. I dictated a letter to John Archer last night. Veronica said they won't be appealing the decision so our job there is done. Please type it up and send it off from my email and let John Archer know we will be sending our final invoice and closing our file on that matter. Also, please get Steve Collins at the Public Prosecutors Office on the line for me."

Josh drank his coffee and looked out at the city coming to life. Now that things had calmed down, maybe he would step up and ask Gabby out on a real date. Make his intentions clear; they had been in that unknown space for too long now. Maybe it was Daniel that complicated matters for her. That must be it. He didn't want to mess up something good, but ultimately their current relationship could only last so long until the inevitable happened – someone wanted more. That someone felt like him at this moment.

The phone rang, showing Shirley's line.

"Mr Carter, I have Steve Collins on the line for you," she said and put him right through.

"Steve, how's the State treating you?"

"Josh! I can't say as good as you. Congratulations on your big win. Our whole office was shocked; they thought it was a slam dunk for the other side. That evidence didn't look good for you and they were sure you wouldn't pull it off, but I told them, 'You don't know my buddy, Josh.'"

"Well, Steve, if I'm honest, I wasn't so sure either."

"I know you're too busy to be calling to have a casual chat. What's up?"

"Steve, I'm just sending feelers out into the water. What is Rhonda Martins up to these days?"

"Wait a minute, did she contact you? Are you on the matter? I am not surprised she has called you in, but Josh, this is big."

"What can you tell me? All I know is she has requested a meeting next week."

"Josh, you know I can't give you official information without it going public first. All I can say is that we have heard the rumours about her setting up a special investigation team for the Hillstrong Holdings matter. Rhonda is going after the execs and everyone else involved. It's going to be the biggest hit of her career and, knowing Rhonda, that means something. You know she's hoping to join the bench. This kind of case would put her right up there for judge nomination. We heard that she was narrowing her options down to the best commercial lawyers. Seems like your last win was what made her decision."

"Alright, I understand that's all you can say. Thanks, Steve. Gives me something to think about."

"You got it, Josh. Good luck."

Now Josh was really day dreaming. Could it really be the Hillstrong Holdings matter? If he was chosen to be a part of the biggest hit of Rhonda Martins' career, it would also be the biggest hit of his own career thus far. Although there couldn't be much money in there, working for the State and all.

Shirley spoke to Josh, giving him a fright. "Mr Carter, did you hear what I said?"

"Sorry, Shirley, I didn't realise you were standing there. What did you say?" His mind was still on his phone call.

"I asked whether you have gone over the briefs for the Russell matter?"

"No, I haven't. I should do that, I need those to go off. Thanks."

Early afternoon came and went and Josh billed and billed his clients. Value for money was his pledge to all his clients. After starting his own firm he had dropped his fees, producing quality work in a very quick turnaround time. He didn't need to inflate his fees or rip off his clients like the big firms did. His overheads were much lower and he only had one other person on the payroll. This seemed to bring in the clients month after month. He didn't even need to advertise much. Old school word of mouth was still the most powerful advertising tool in the legal industry. He took part in the occasional golf day and attended all the business and networking functions, more for being a part of it and not for touting for work.

He was done for the day. Traffic leaving Sandton would be a nightmare at this time, despite him not living too far away. He would walk to Isabelle's and have a drink and a chat to Vee, if she wasn't too busy although, when it came to Josh, she never was.

Isabelle's was packed, as it usually was, even on a week night. Vivian saw Josh walk in the door and watched him make his way across the room. She stood behind the counter, and gazed over at him as he made his way closer to her. She knew that no one would ever replace the husband that she had lost, but Josh had a very special place in her heart. She had come to know him quite well. They had become close after all the nights of having drinks and chatting, sometimes early into the morning. She waved him over and sat him down in the secluded booth where they always sat together. It was almost as if she kept that booth open in the event that Josh would arrive unannounced. The booth had dim lights and a waiter on hand.

"Hey, Vee. Figured I would have a midweek drink and say hello, if you're not busy," he said.

"Perfect timing, I was about to fix myself a drink while the late shift takes over for the dinner arrangements."

She poured them both a glass of Pinotage, sat back and looked into his eyes, the way she always did, in such an endearing and affectionate way. He told her all about the case that had just finished. They spoke about life and love and everything in-between.

"Any love interests that I don't know about?" Vee asked him.

"Gabby and I have been spending time together; nothing more has progressed though. You should meet her; she's great!" he said.

"Bring her by the restaurant some time. I would love to meet her," said Vivian.

"I will, soon. What about you, Vee? There must be plenty of wealthy businessmen passing through your restaurant on a daily basis. Anybody you find to be of interest?"

"There are, but they think money can make me see past the arrogance and shallow views they have about women. They are so entitled because they have had a small taste of success. To get involved with men like that only to be traded in for a younger model would be a waste of time." She placed a hand on Josh's arm and slowly moved it away again.

When Vivian's husband had died, she'd closed herself off to men, except Josh. She had taken a liking to him like to no other man. Isabelle's had become her life. She took such pride in her restaurant and it was clear to everyone how much passion and effort she put into the place. It was the most popular place for lawyers, businessmen, the city guys.

The restaurant filled up, then quietened down, and slowly the evening dinner reservations were leaving. The chairs were placed onto the tables and the floors were cleaned while Vee and Josh continued to chat away.

"I'd better leave otherwise I won't make it home tonight," he said.

"If you want to spend the night upstairs, you are welcome to!" she said. Vivian had a modern, furnished bachelor pad above the restaurant that she used when she had functions and didn't feel like driving home. Josh had used it in the past when he had had too much to drink, one time with Vivian but mostly on his own.

Josh felt fine to drive, but knew he was over the limit. He didn't want to complicate things between him and Vivian, despite the one night they'd shared in the past, especially since he was drawing closer to Gabby.

It had been a while since he'd stayed over at Vee's upstairs pad and even though he had been drinking he decided he would risk driving; hopefully the cops weren't out on his route home. Josh kissed Vee on the cheek and embraced her tightly. She held onto him longer than a friend would have.

The walk back to the office wasn't long. A man stood under a street-light on the opposite side of the road. Was this the same man who had been standing outside Carter & Associates earlier? The man wore a cap but no jacket. Josh couldn't be sure if it was the same man or not. He tried to think whether he had seen that man standing there when he'd arrived at Isabelle's but decided that maybe he was being paranoid. First an unusual meeting request and now he was imagining people were keeping tabs on him. It was probably just an Uber driver having a smoke before accepting his next ride.

On his way home, he saw the police roadblock. "Shit. Just my luck. This is all I need right now." He drove up slowly towards the cops; they waved him closer with their flash-lights and asked him to pull over. "I should have just stayed over at Vee's."

"Good evening, sir," said the officer holding his flashlight and shining it into Josh's car.

"Good evening, officer," said Josh.

"Have you been drinking tonight, sir?"

"I had a glass of wine a bit earlier," said Josh casually, which wasn't entirely true; he had had three.

"Please may I have your driver's licence, sir?" asked the officer. Josh took his licence out of his wallet and handed it to the policeman. The policeman took the licence and walked back to his patrol car. It wasn't two minutes later and the policeman was back at his car window. "Shit, he's going to ask me for a breathalyzer." But instead the officer said, "You may go, sir. Drive safely." The policeman handed Josh his licence and walked away to pull over the next car driving up the road. That was close! Josh wasn't about to complain. He would go home and sleep soundly.

CHAPTER FIVE

Ranch House

Josh wanted to, at least, take the meeting with Rhonda Martins. If it were something he did not want to get involved in for reputational or any other reasons, he would just walk away from it. He had to consider whether working for the State against big corporates might deter other big corporates from using his services.

Shirley called Rhonda and accepted the meeting invite and only upon acceptance of the meeting did he receive the details of where and when it would take place.

**

He was on his way, in his BMW, to a private game lodge in KwaZulu-Natal, south of the Swaziland border. It was about a four hour drive. It was clear that the Public Prosecutor wanted the meeting to remain discreet. He took the N17 highway out of the city and the buildings faded in his review mirror. The roads were double lanes with plenty of visual distance to see any trouble, so he let the BMW loose.

After two and a half hours he was driving through the forestry where the paper companies were chopping, stripping and loading large logs. He arrived at the turn off for the game lodge on the Mkuze River and wished he hadn't had to drive his sports car on the gravel road. He checked the directions that he had written down by hand, as he had been told the sat-nav wouldn't pick up the location – not only because it was in the middle of nowhere, but because the government had paid Google to remove it from Google Maps and every other direction-assisting app that could be downloaded on smartphones these days. A person could do that.

He pulled up to the lodge gate where a guard was stationed. "Please wait here sir, as I phone ahead," he said to Josh in his deep, masculine voice. Josh nodded in obedience. The guard wasn't the usual reserve gate-keeper; the large gun he was holding was no hunting rifle, well at least, not for hunting animals. The guard was fully kitted out with a sniper rifle, sidearm, Kevlar vest, and other things strapped to him that Josh didn't want to know about. This was a contractor who had obviously served in the army's Special Forces.

What was he getting himself into? Could this really be a precaution because of the Hillstrong Holdings matter? he wondered to himself. He was asked to drive over a grid and get out of the vehicle so that two further guards stationed at the gate, whom he hadn't even seen, could search his car all around, even underneath. Once they were satisfied that he was not smuggling in any dangerous weapons, explosives or other electronic equipment, he was permitted to proceed.

"Go straight and keep going until you reach the Ranch House," the guard instructed him. Josh gave the Special Forces contractor a salute and hoped it didn't offend him. He drove a further five kilometres on the dirt road before seeing any buildings. He saw giraffe, nyala and plenty of warthogs. He reminded himself to tell

Daniel that he had seen Pumba. South Africa has the best wildlife and nature reserves in the world and, if it weren't for the suspicious undertone of his visit, it could have felt like a holiday. Also, he was dressed like a lawyer in the heat and humid weather of a game farm in KwaZulu-Natal.

He pulled up at what was called "The Ranch House" in brass lettering on a wooden plaque. It was more like a mansion on the outskirts of Texas, and not a venue a few hours outside of Johannesburg. The mansion was a double storey. It had huge glass windows with stone cladding on all the walls, water features and well maintained gardens. The building was situated on the side of a mountain overlooking the Mkuze River.

He imagined a retired president living in a place like this, out in the middle of nowhere but with all the luxuries money could buy. It was odd seeing something so luxurious out in nature, yet it also seemed quite fitting – the architecture suited the setting perfectly.

Josh parked the BMW next to three black Range Rovers with government plates, a police cruiser, a game drive vehicle with seats for tourists, and a farm bakkie.

He climbed out of his BMW and walked towards the Ranch House. Two big bodyguards in suits stepped forward the moment he reached the wooden deck leading to the front entrance. He hadn't even seen them standing there, taking the form of two pillars next to the front door to the mansion.

"Raise your arms and spread your legs," said the pillar on the left. Josh did what he was told while they searched him. It seemed like they were searching for more than just a weapon, probably a wire or recorder of some sort.

He entered the lodge-type mansion and it was even more impressive than he'd imagined from the outside. High ceilings, state of the art appliances and flat screen TVs; the occasional animal head on the wall, fireplaces, and a modern kitchen, all open plan. This was something Josh could work the rest of his life for; he had found his goal for retirement. In the room past the living area was the most expensive leather suite and accompanying furniture, a boardroom with fully equipped conference facilities including video and projector.

In the boardroom sat Public Prosecutor, Rhonda Martins, and someone who appeared to be a detective solely by the look of his moustache, and further bodyguards. The cars out front gave the characters away too. The boardroom was a large room with floor-to-ceiling fold-up glass doors that opened onto a wooden deck boasting the view from the mountainside and over the river below.

Rhonda Martins greeted Josh. "Mr Carter, thank you for joining us today. We apologise for making you travel so far out of your way and for the invasive searches on your way in to the Ranch House. Before we make any introductions, I would ask you to place all electronic devices in this solid case." She pointed to a bomb-proof case designed to block all signal once a phone or tablet device was placed inside. He did so and waited for her to proceed.

"I am joined by Detective Mark Sidd from the Commercial Crimes division of investigations." She pulled out her briefcase and slid a piece of paper over the desk to him and informed him that if he wished to proceed with the introductory meeting he was required to sign a confidentiality and non-disclosure agreement. He had obviously seen and drafted many of these in his life. The terms were pretty standard until he got to the breach clause – it provided that, instead of a financial penalty, should he breach his confidentiality undertakings he would be charged criminally for obstruction of justice and treason, with a life sentence of prison time at stake. He looked up at Rhonda and she answered his look without waiting for the question.

"Yes, it's extreme, but unfortunately that is the level that we are playing at at the moment."

"I can't sign a document with such grave consequences without knowing what I am getting myself into," he said.

"All I can say is that we are investigating the Hillstrong Holdings matter. I'm sure you are up to date with the matter in the news at the very least. The investigation will include wealthy businessman and, from the information that we have received from our sources, these people don't like to play fair. The people whom we are investigating do not take kindly to anyone becoming involved in their business other than for reasons of profit.

"You will be glad to hear that the State has thrown all its resources at this investigation: financial, staff, networking, equipment, the works. The team will be kept small. Everyone part of it has been thoroughly vetted with background checks and we have been keeping tabs."

Josh interpreted it as, "We have been following you around for quite some time. He remembered the man outside his office and Isabelle's.

"The files are confidential under the Secrecy Act. Even government officials not participating in this matter will not be able to view them." That was little assurance for him.

"What else do I need to know?"

"We will require your full co-operation and availability. And you do not need to worry about the financial consequences of that. We are prepared to pay triple your hourly rate for the work that you put in, full day fees on retainer until further notice, and bonus incentives for milestones that we reach.

"For example, if we successfully prosecute the people on our list you will receive a large bonus. And if you continue with the meeting we will also get rid of the speeding fine you received by the camera on the way here today. We've already let you past our road block the other night when it was clear you had had a few too many. Typically, you would be entitled to certain benefits, not quite the extent of diplomatic immunity but when it comes to misdemeanours like traffic offences we can turn a blind eye."

Josh did not know what to say. This was going to be one of the most important decisions he would ever have to make and there was a part of him that didn't really think they would take no for an answer either. His legal career was about to take off into the history books. Josh then did something that would change his life forever. He signed the document and said, "I'm in."

Rhonda and Detective Sidd began the briefing session.

"We are going to give you the background and history of the corporate giant known to the world as Hillstrong Holdings," said Rhonda, as she used a remote to switch on a projector and lower a white canvas from the ceiling. "The Hillstrong Holdings scandal could turn out to be the biggest case of corporate fraud in South African business history, maybe even the world. Over the past few weeks the company's share price collapse has dominated the news internationally.

"Wikus Louw is the newly resigned CEO of the Hillstrong group of companies. However, the story does not start with him. The founder of Hillstrong Holdings, German Karl Helmut, founded the company in 1960. Over a period of roughly sixty years, the group of companies has expanded to what is now referred to as one of the largest furniture retail groups in the world."

The slides that Rhonda had prepared were now being shown on the white screen by the projector. The first slide was a portrait of Karl Helmut as he looked today, and a much younger picture taken sixty years earlier. The next slide was a world map showing where Hillstrong companies had a presence. Josh counted at least eight different countries with multiple jurisdictions in each country. She changed the slide, showing a map of Germany.

"In the early 60s, the company started out as a business that sold household goods in Germany, selling cheap furniture made in one side of the country, with a high mark-up to the more established side of the country. Hillstrong become a very lucrative business. It was this core principle that ensured the growth leading to Hillstrong becoming the renowned company that it is today," said Rhonda Martins. She walked to the back of the room, opened a cupboard and retrieved two writing pads and pens and slid them across the table to each of Josh and Detective Sidd.

"Thanks," said Josh. "So we already have two persons of interest – Wikus Louw and Karl Helmut – I assume? A corporation of that size, with the reputations of each of those men, would mean that they would always have a finger on the pulse."

"Correct," answered Rhonda and merely smiled at Detective Sidd when he winked at her in an I-told-you-he-is-the-right-guy look. She continued with her briefing. "Karl Helmut had a gift for selling furniture and household goods, together with his work ethic, determination and entrepreneurial spirit.

"Like many successful entrepreneurs, Karl Helmut came from humble beginnings. He started off working from home out of a spare room. Soon he was able to rent a small warehouse, enabling the paperwork and manual labour to be under one roof. He had that warehouse stocked with furniture, as much as the space would allow. He invested everything he had into his business." Rhonda showed black and white pictures of furniture warehouses in Germany.

"He slept in that warehouse, and when there wasn't enough space, because he had filled that warehouse to the brim, he slept in his car. He was relentless. He was not only superb at selling products, he was prepared to venture to areas his competitors were not prepared to go. Whether it was a war zone or an undeveloped area, there was no place he was not willing to reach out to in order to sell his furniture.

"Karl Helmut was able to network with numerous powerful people. This assisted him in building a well-known brand in political, economic and social circles. This start to the life of the Hillstrong business was vital for its survival over the years."

Rhonda paused to order the three of them lunch. Three salmon salads were already prepared and waiting for them and were brought into the conference room. She spoke while she ate.

"Despite the Cold War escalating, Karl Helmut was determined to take advantage of all business opportunities and grow his business. He crossed borders and ventured into new territories at a rapid rate, in commercial terms, and before the 1980s he was sourcing furniture from all parts from Germany, Denmark, Italy, the Netherlands, and even Russia." The slides depicted each country as Rhonda mentioned them.

"Although he was doing extremely well as a furniture retailer, Karl decided to become a furniture manufacturer as well. This was all part of the greater plan to grow his business and own the entire supply chain. The strong economic growth in Europe was great for the demand for furniture that Karl wholly took advantage of. He constructed factories to keep up with the demand. They manufactured different products backed by a brand of quality and the reputation Karl Helmut has always prided himself with.

"If it weren't for his aggressive and bold business decisions, he might not have survived the global recession in the late 1980s. He was even able to provide products to the tight-wallet consumers. Despite having to operate under tough economic conditions, he continued to expand and grow by exporting his products to other countries of the world. His big break came from his relationship with companies in China."

The slide now showed a map of China and pictures of the various cargo trains with German men offloading large crates of supplies for manufacturing furniture.

"Hillstrong became one of the first companies to import from China. One of the oldest standing relationships between the Hillstrong Holdings companies and other furniture businesses is with the Chinese corporations. There were rumours of partnerships in those years, but it was said that Karl Helmut would never share the glory or the wealth with any other companies. He either offered to acquire you or he put you out of business. There we see the aggressive business principles again.

"In the 1980s, his revenue was in the hundreds of millions, his employee count had entered the hundreds and the company kept pumping capital back into the business to expand. Further factories and storage facilities were built, costing tens of millions euros.

"The fall of the Iron Curtain in November 1989 presented the company with a massive opportunity for expansion in Europe. This new era lifted all restrictions on trade for goods and services across all borders, allowing exponential growth in Germany. Even the German government offered business incentives to invest in the country as opposed to internationally. Hillstrong Holdings dominated the business sphere and absorbed any competitor attempting to supply or manufacture goods and services in the furniture industry.

"At that time, Hillstrong purchased some factories manufacturing upholstery products and even bedding. Karl Helmut put as much capital into the businesses as was required, resulting in Hillstrong Holdings becoming the largest producer in the German market. He made various important investments in trading companies that would take his product even further, to France and Austria. By the 1990s, Hillstrong Holdings experienced revenue of over half a billion euros."

The slides changed to the map of South Africa, more particularly the Cape and then Johannesburg.

"The next big time-frame occurred from the mid-nineties to 2012, when he entered South Africa. With the end of the apartheid era and the lifting of the international sanctions against South Africa in the early 90s, many international companies wanted to invest in our country. The investment personnel working for Hillstrong Holdings decided to invest in a manufacturer of middle and upper class household furniture. This was the crucial point where Wikus Louw crossed paths with Karl Helmut." A large portrait of Wikus Louw was displayed on the white screen; one that oozed wealth and success at a lavish looking business function.

"Wikus and Karl became friends through an investment transaction in a company that Wikus was working for. Back in those days he was an accountant, one with much higher ambitions. After this investment, Hillstrong Holdings consisted of two main business divisions – Hillstrong Europe and Hillstrong Africa. Each was focused on one goal: to control the entire supply chain, from manufacturing to logistics activities of the business. One of the strategic moves made by Hillstrong Africa was opening a sourcing office in China. Wikus Louw has been the CEO of the Hillstrong group of companies for the past fifteen years.

"Since his appointment to the present day, the Hillstrong Holdings group of companies has acquired an incredible number of multi-million Rand businesses. For any internationally recognised business, one major acquisition transaction a year or over a few years is considered an enormous feat. Hillstrong Holdings had years where it acquired five or six businesses worth billions of Rand in total. Mid-year last year, Hillstrong Holdings had a market capitalization of over R250 billion.

"Over the days that followed the resignation of Wikus Louw, the share price of Hillstrong Holdings took a dive off a cliff. The public company sent out a SENS announcement that it had become aware of 'accounting irregularities' and that the auditors were refusing to sign off the financial statements. I'm sure that, by following the news of the past few weeks, you know what happened from there. Investment firms, pension funds, government bodies all lost billions of Rands. It is our job to determine the extent of the 'irregularities' and the parties involved. Whether or not this crosses the South African border and so on.

"Currently, the company faces investigations and legal action instituted by numerous bodies and authorities, including the Johannesburg Stock Exchange, the Financial Services Board, the Department of Trade and Industry, and the Companies and Intellectual Property Commission. The company is also facing two different class action lawsuits in Germany and the Netherlands.

"The search and seizure operation that took place at Hillstrong Holdings offices revealed that many of the offices have been cleared out and that boxes of paperwork have been moved off-site. The operation at Wikus Louw's home was, however, a lucky break. Mark did incredibly well and obtained vital documentary evidence which it will be your job to review, Josh. Mark, we are still waiting for the electronic files to be decrypted and uploaded to the secure server, is that correct?" she asked Detective Sidd.

"Yes, I'll let you guys know as soon as the Commercial Crimes Division's IT department is done there. I am also waiting for the outsourced company's details that removed all the documents off the premises of Hillstrong Holdings so that we can follow up that lead as well."

"Josh, if you would prefer to spend the night, there are plenty of rooms available. That goes for any time during the investigation. If you feel like a change of scenery we have the place to ourselves," said Rhonda.

"Thank you, perhaps next time."

CHAPTER SIX

Pre-Investigation

On Saturday morning, most people were sleeping, except for Josh who was out on his Ducati again, going for a breakfast run. On a breakfast run bikers woke up early on the weekend, met at a designated place, if they were part of a club, and then rode together to a breakfast joint, a popular hangout for bike riders with a buffet breakfast – not the dirty looking, long bearded, tattooed type of bikers, but the full leathered, superbike riders. Sometimes it would be just a well-known Wimpy branch and other times specific biker lodges on the outskirts of the city.

He would often see other bikers on the road and when he came up next to another rider who was riding in the same direction, it became a race. That was the unspoken rule for individual riders and often smaller bike clubs riding together. The larger group of riders often rode together and did not chase the bait of a non-club member speeding past them.

When it came to bikes, it didn't matter what bike you rode, if you were out on your bike early morning, you were one of them. You didn't have to wear colours or club badges to be respected on the road by other bikers. This was something Josh had realised early on when taking these bike rides. That other riders always acknowledged each other, out of respect. It was a form of brotherhood, which wasn't restricted to men either.

When riding past another biker going in the opposite direction, there would be a brief moment, a second, where both riders would acknowledge and nod their helmet to the other. The biker's nod, he called it. In the same way that gentlemen would tip their top hats to other men in the street back in the day. It was almost as if they would tell each other, "I see you, I respect your passion for riding, and be safe out there". He very seldom rode past a biker who didn't perform the biker's nod. The bike circles that Josh found himself in were the adrenalin junkies. The ones that said "Life starts at 300km/h".

That morning Josh was riding solo, as usual. He had already come across one or two other riders who wanted to test him, to see who had the bigger balls. It got more and more risky and dangerous the longer the race endured. Josh would split two cars at an idiotic speed if he had to get past, or overtake on the inside and even go around on the outside of the yellow line. Rules of the road went out the window. The only rule was winning.

There were very few riders that stuck it out with Josh when the challenge was accepted. He would hold out just that little bit longer than most at high speed. At the point where doubt entered the other rider's mind, he would accelerate and the other rider, with his life at risk, would admit defeat and slack off instantaneously.

When Josh had been a young boy, he'd used to ride pillion with his father. His father was fearless on the bike. Being such a large man, he needed the largest and most powerful road bike available. The Suzuki Hayabusa GSX1300R was known as having the reputation of the king of the road with the well-known slogan, "If you aren't on it, you're behind it".

Josh's arms would be wrapped tightly around his father's waist and other riders would challenge them to a race. His father would reach down and pull Josh's hands tighter around his waist as the signal to hold on tight and, without hesitation, the accelerator would be opened, releasing power from zero to hero in seconds. The other riders, without any passengers, would hang on for as long as they could until ultimately they would slack off the power and fade into the distance. Josh would hold onto his father, trusting him completely. If his father leaned to take the bend, he would lean with him.

When Josh turned twenty-two, he bought his first motorcycle, a Suzuki 1200cc, a cross between speed and comfort. It was powerful. He wondered if he would ever be able to ride a bike the way his father did. The older he got, and after an accident that could have cost his life although he was lucky just to break a leg, he was more aware of the dangers of riding. Once doubt entered his mind, he became its prisoner. It had taken years to get his bravery back. Or was it stupidity?

Josh arrived at the breakfast place, the sun barely up. The air was fresh, and there were at least twenty other bikes parked, some guys smoking, others having a coffee and a hot breakfast. He paid for his breakfast buffet, dished up a plate of eggs, bacon, toast, beans, fried tomato and a cheese griller sausage, and sat outside at a wooden table under a tree. He could hear the screaming sound of a bike engine in the distance, either on its way to this breakfast spot or onwards to another.

He was under strict instructions not to involve anyone else in the investigation unless agreed and formally vetted, although he was sure that they had already done a background check on Shirley. He let out a slight chuckle, wondering what they would find on someone like his secretary. He then thought about Gabby. He wanted to make it official and hopefully in the near future ask her and Daniel to move in with him. He would arrange a babysitter for Daniel, and take her on a date to Isabelle's. But that might put too much pressure on the situation. He could casually bring it up when they were together and play it cool. No, that would seem like he hadn't thought about it enough when clearly he had thought about it plenty.

Over-thinking was his thing. Although in his line of work it wasn't a bad thing. He would take her on a date, next weekend.

Josh felt his phone vibrate in his leather jacket's pocket. It was an update text from Detective Sidd, informing him of the date for the next briefing session at the Ranch House. The message stated that the search and seizure team would be uploading all the documentary evidence onto a secure server. There Josh would be able to view all of the evidence confiscated from Wikus Louw's home. For the time being, Detective Sidd and Rhonda Martins had set up a secure cloud drive for Josh to view all the photographs taken by the forensic photographer. The seized documents would be uploaded and accompanied by a description of where in the house they were located.

Taking the bike rides made him realise how much he needed a holiday. He hadn't taken one over the previous December break because of his ongoing trial, and now it seemed that he would not be having one for a long time. He would ask Shirley to keep a reminder on his calendar; the first opportunity he got he would take a trip. Perhaps he would ask Gabby and Daniel to join him. He grabbed his helmet and climbed back on his bike. On his way home, hoping for a challenge, he passed two riders, but they were going in the opposite direction. Both riders gave him the biker's nod. He pulled into his street and accelerated, wondering if Daniel was watching through the window. He was, waving hysterically. Josh gave him the nod as if he were a rider himself. Josh parked his bike and hung up his jacket. Gabby walked across the road into his garage.

"Hey, Josh," she shouted, almost out of breath.

"Hey Gabs, everything alright?" he replied.

"I have a huge favour to ask of you. I have to show a house this morning. It's a big one, really hoping it pulls through. Would you be able to watch Daniel for me for a while?"

"Yes, sure. I was planning on going to the gym so I'll take him with so he can play at the play area while I'm working out," he said.

"Perfect. You're a life saver! I owe you one!" she said, already on her way back across the road to fetch Daniel.

"You can make it up to me next Saturday night for dinner," he quickly added.

She turned around and smiled. "It's a deal! I'll bring him over in ten minutes."

Josh changed into his sweat vest, shorts and trainers for gym and met Gabby and Daniel out front.

***

Josh and Daniel were outside by the pool when Gabby returned. She walked through the house to where the boys were and then slowed when she approached. She looked at Josh through the lounge window. He was wearing only board shorts and sunglasses. His chest and biceps were bulging from the gym session. She took a deep breath to catch herself and then remembered her good news.

"I did it! I sold it! It was the double-storey on Fifth Avenue. It was touch and go for a while but I convinced them that they would be making a great investment that couldn't be passed up!"

"That's fantastic, Gabs, well done! We should celebrate! Now you can start looking for a house for me!" said Josh. He had been thinking about up-sizing for a while now and, if he wanted a family – actually, his thoughts were if he wanted Gabby and Daniel to eventually move in with him – he would need a bigger place.

"Really?" Gabby said excitedly.

"Definitely. I've been considering it for a while now and who better to trust than you!" he said.

"What are you looking for?" she asked, already talking business.

"Something modern. Three, maybe four rooms, two baths, splash pool, with more garden space, an office... something like this but just bigger and better," he added with his boyish smile.

Gabby sat on one of the deck chairs with her mind racing. She was still focused on Josh without his shirt on but now also on the fact that she had a new client. "I already have two houses that I think you might like, pricey but right up your alley! The sellers are moving out in a few weeks, I'll let you know as soon as I set them up for show. You can have first right of refusal," she said and winked at him. "Perks of knowing people."

CHAPTER SEVEN

Networking Event

A<small>T AROUND</small> 6<small>PM</small> J<small>OSH TEXTED</small> Gabby to let her know that the Uber driver had arrived to fetch them. In return for watching Daniel, Josh had called in the favour that she owed. He'd asked her to be his date to his annual networking event at the Sandton City Convention Centre.

He walked out the garage onto the street towards Gabby's, where the Uber driver had parked the black Mercedes C Class with chrome finish – Uber Black, obviously. There was a light breeze keeping Josh pleasantly cool in his black tux and bow-tie. He was busy chatting to the Uber driver through the driver window when Gabby's front door opened and she emerged, wearing a black cocktail dress, black heels, and her brown hair half up in a bun with curls hanging down to her right shoulder. Her dress was tight enough to show off the curves of her body and her athletic legs. Both men said nothing but watched Gabby walk to the car.

The Uber driver was first to break his stare and save the moment.

"Are you going to open the car door for the lady?" whispered the Uber driver so that only Josh could hear.

Josh felt like he was waiting for his date at his High School farewell. He opened the back door of the Uber and waited for Gabby. "You look incredible, Gabs."

"You clean up pretty nicely yourself."

Gabby and Josh gazed at each other in the back of the Mercedes; the Uber driver snuck a glance as well, They drove into Sandton as the sunset reflected off the glass buildings in the city, illuminating the streets and cars ahead with an orange glow.

"The city is quite beautiful at this time of day." She admired the view.

"It has its hustle and bustle every day, but it's these quiet moments, when traffic dies down, that you really appreciate the beauty of the buildings and the principle of where you are. Sandton is the richest square mile in the country," he said, looking up at his office windows as they drove past.

"So what must I expect tonight? Is this where you get new business and network with colleagues?" she asked.

She was so beautiful, calm, and just so perfect, Josh thought. He didn't really care much for the business side of the evening any more, which was unlike him.

"Something like that. I don't really advertise for work, I've been very fortunate in that way. Word of mouth has provided enough to keep me busy for the last five years. It's just good to be kept on the invite list with the people with power, if that makes sense. Let's just have a good time, okay?"

They arrived at the Sandton Convention Centre and exited the car after a valet opened the door for them. The place was decorated for the rich and famous, just like any charity ball that the rich folk would attend. They entered the hall. White drapes hung from the centre of the high ceiling's crystal chandelier, adorned with fairy lights. The tables were all identically set up with white tablecloths and silverware. Each table had an exquisite bouquet of flowers and crystals, with different wines chilled in ice buckets.

It was a seated affair. Josh and Gabby would be sitting with the public prosecutor, and some very wealthy businessmen, some lawyers and the mayor of Sandton, along with their respective partners. There was a live jazz band in the corner providing background music. On arrival, one of the many smartly dressed waiters offered them a glass of champagne that they both gladly accepted.

"To a night for us," Josh said and clinked Gabby's glass. She looked at him adoringly and took his arm as they walked around the room. Josh introduced her to the more important personalities in the room, one by one. Many commented on how beautiful she was and jokingly asked what on earth Josh had done to deserve an angel when he was a lawyer, the scum of the earth. She played the game back at them so smoothly, handling herself in powerful company in a way that amazed him.

"It's not what he has done right to deserve me, Mayor, but what I have done wrong to be stuck with him," she joked, and everyone laughed, even Josh. He was in a happy place. The night was surely going to be a very memorable one.

They all stood around to listen to the Mayor for the introduction and announcements of the evening.

"Good evening, ladies and gentlemen. Welcome to our annual networking event. Tonight is a night where we are all appreciative of our good fortune and use this opportunity to forge new relationships to increase that good fortune. Most importantly, the whole purpose of the event is to assist the less fortunate at the same time. All proceeds of this event are being donated to five different charities whose representatives will be going around the room later with pledge cards for you to commit a small fortune over the period of the remaining months of the year." Everyone clapped politely and walked around to find their seats.

On the table was a four course menu. For starters they were having calamari tubes complemented by a rich white wine and garlic sauce. Thereafter, as a further appetizer, they could taste the pea soup with freshly baked rolls. The main course was a choice of duck, fish or beef all prepared with their own sides to complement the main dish. For dessert there was home-made nougat ice cream.

Throughout dinner the table conversation naturally covered politics, business and jokes, often at Josh's expense or whichever other lawyer was nearby. Gabby and Rhonda Martins hit it off extremely well. At one point, although Josh was involved in a different conversation, he noticed that Rhonda offered her card to Gabby, saying that if she ever needed anything she should call, and that hopefully they could go out and have a drink when her hectic schedule offered an opening. It would be nice to have lady time away from work, Rhonda had said.

Josh and Gabby drank, laughed, danced, and drank some more. They went to the bar to rest their feet.

"I'm off to the men's room. Don't let any of these dirty old men take you away from me," Josh said as he got up to leave.

"In that case, you had better not take too long," she played. "The Mayor is recently divorced and – I didn't know this before tonight – I may have a thing for curly, grey moustaches."

They had been flirting the entire night. When dancing together their hands on each other had felt so good and she'd held him so affectionately, lovingly. Josh had forgotten how amazing it felt to have such a beautiful woman with him for a night of good fun. One with whom he could have a conversation; someone with a mind as beautiful as her looks. And her body... wow, it made Josh feel stupid.

He returned to two mixed drinks at the bar for him and Gabby.

"Any trouble from these guys that I should know about?" he asked.

"No, luckily not," she said.

"This looks interesting, cheers!"

"Cheers!" Gabby looked into his blue eyes and put her hand on his leg. He felt the blood rush all over his body, especially down there. She had sex appeal, confidence and, damn, she looked so good tonight. They talked some more, laughed some more, and watched all the people around them.

The DJ made an announcement. "Ladies and gentlemen, I will be playing the last song for the evening, a slow one for all the lovers out there tonight."

They downed their drinks and walked onto the dance floor. Josh was feeling the night's fun catching up with him. Gabby held him close enough for him to smell her perfume mixed with sweat. He felt his adrenalin rush from holding her so close, her skin so soft. She put her arms around him as they danced. The looks she gave him, with that naughty smile of hers that he hadn't seen before tonight... Could life get any better than this moment right here? "This is what I have been missing," Josh thought. They didn't say anything to each other for the whole song, just held each other while they moved over the dance floor together.

"Let's get out of here," Josh said, and led her outside. The organisers of the event had sponsored metered taxis for the drive home so that no-one at an event that consisted of so many lawyers and government officials, would have to break the very laws that they worked so hard to enforce. They climbed into the back of the taxi cab. Josh gave his address and the taxi pulled out into the street for the drive home.

The window was open, Gabby's long brown hair was blowing in the cool breeze. He could still smell her perfume and her sweet scent of perspiration. He took her hand and she stared at him, then leaned over and kissed him deeply. There was that blood flow again, the power a woman had over a man. It was irresistible, like the feeling of power, the confidence to take on the world. The car felt as though it was spinning. Was that the alcohol or Gabby? Probably a bit of both. He didn't know, nor did he care.

The taxi pulled up to the cul de sac and into Josh's driveway. The driver wished them a good evening and left. Josh stepped inside the front entrance of his home and, before he had closed the door or switched on the lights, Gabby pulled him closer and kissed him again. They ran their hands all over each other. She removed his jacket and his bow-tie and then they were kissing and stumbling around the room, partly because of the alcohol and partly because of the darkness. He switched on a dim lamp so they could stop bumping into everything and see each other without ruining the mood.

He started taking off her dress but she stopped him. "I know this is bad timing, but I need the ladies. I'll be right back, I promise. Don't go anywhere," she said with a naughty smile and bit her lip as she walked away from him.

Josh put on some soft music in the background. Suddenly he did not feel so great. How much had he had to drink? He stood at the kitchen counter trying to remember the last time he'd had such a great night.

Gabby returned. Her hair was now loose and she was wearing only black lace underwear. Her body was fit and toned. She did a little turn for Josh; she wore a thong showing off her firm bottom. Her confidence exuded sexiness.

"Wow, gorgeous," he said, staring at her half-naked body. He battled to stand.

"Are you alright, Josh? You don't look so good. You're very pale," Gabby said.

Not wanting to ruin the moment Josh brushed it off and pulled her towards him. "I'm fine, just think I had a bit too much to drink. I'm used to the whiskey, just not the mix drinks that you ordered us," he said. He was feeling very confused and he'd started to slur his words.

"I didn't order any drinks, I thought you had," she said. Josh wasn't sure what she was saying because the room was spinning.

"I need to sit down." Josh tried to find the chair with his hand reaching out but instead fell flat onto the floor, knocking his head on a side-table and smashing a lamp.

Gabby couldn't lift him. "Josh! Oh no! Josh! Something is wrong. I think someone spiked your drink!"

Josh could hear her words but nothing was making any sense. He couldn't move, he was finding it difficult to breathe, his body was numb, he felt paralysed, and his vision was a blur. Gabby was rummaging through her handbag, looking for something while frantically calling out to him. She was on the phone to someone, his eardrums were going in and out of hearing.

"Josh, help is on the way, hold on, please Josh!"

He looked at her. It was like a movie. She was talking so fast and he could hear nothing. He saw her facial expressions through tunnel vision, but did not know what was going on. She was crying and holding his face, but his eyes couldn't stay open for any longer.

"Josh, please be okay. I love you so much! Please!"

Josh shook violently and foamed at the mouth. Two men in paramedic's uniforms burst through the door and knelt down next to him on the floor, flashing a light into his eyes. One of the men restrained a screaming and crying Gabby. At that point he lost consciousness.

CHAPTER EIGHT

Aftermath

JOSH WOKE UP IN A hospital room, hooked up to a whole range of machines and with a plaster on the side of his face where they'd stitched the wound on his head caused by hitting the side table. He was alone in his own room. Gabby's jacket hung over the back of a chair next to his bed. There was also a BMW M4 model car at the foot of his bed, which he had given to Daniel for his last birthday. Gabby and Daniel had been there; maybe they had stepped out to get something to eat. He felt like death warmed up. He could, although with great difficulty and pain, at least move his muscles now.

A nurse walked in. "Mr Carter, you're awake," she said. "I'll go get the doctor." She left immediately. In a few minutes the door opened again and Gabby and Daniel entered the room.

"Josh!" Gabby burst into tears and ran to his bed and hugged him. Daniel hugged him too.

"What happened?" Josh asked.

"You were poisoned at the networking event, but the poison only set in when we got home. The doctor said that you were almost too far gone to save. They can't believe that you held on for so long. You gave me such a fright."

She had dark rings under her eyes and wasn't wearing much make-up. She obviously hadn't slept much and she had been crying. Daniel also looked upset.

"Hey bud, how you doing?" he asked Daniel.

"Fine, thanks. Glad you're okay, Josh," he said and hugged him.

"Me too, bud."

The door opened again. This time it was the doctor. He and the nurse who had gone to fetch him walked over to the bed. "Mr Carter, you are one very lucky man. I haven't seen such a deadly dose of poison in one man's system and have him live to tell the tale. The substance is very intriguing as well, of Chinese or Japanese origin; we haven't narrowed the source down to which one yet. Our research tells us that a substance similar to this was used during the Second Sino-Japanese War, which was a military conflict fought primarily between the Republic of China and the Empire of Japan." The doctor checked Josh's pulse, removed a pen from the front pocket of his white coat and held it in front of Josh's eyes and told him to follow it while flashing a light into his pupils.

"You are going to be feeling like a zombie for a few days. That is because you were practically dead and brought back to life again. We also pumped your stomach, but you will be okay. If this young lady over here," he gestured towards Gabby, "hadn't acted as quickly as she did to get you help, you wouldn't be here anymore. I'm talking about one more minute, Mr Carter."

Gabby's eyes were still full of tears as she held Daniel in her arms. "We want to keep you here for at least another day and check your vitals before discharging you. I will be back later this afternoon and will pop in while doing my rounds. You need to get as much rest as possible." The doctor and the nurse left.

"So, I owe you my life, literally. Thank you, Gabs," Josh said sincerely.

She was still quite emotional. "I am just glad you are alive. I don't know what I, what we, would do without you," she said as she moved closer to his bed, climbed on the side of it and lay next to him with her arm over his chest. Daniel sat on the floor and played with his model car.

"Rhonda was here with Detective Sidd. They mentioned that their office had received death threats. They don't have many leads but are opening an investigation into it. They suspect that it's related to the new matter that you are working on with them. Josh, what have you gotten yourself into?" She looked concerned.

"I am as surprised as you are. I didn't think it would lead to something like this. Unfortunately, now that I am in, there is no getting out until the job is done." He paused and tried to think of what had happened the night before, but he was finding it difficult to focus. "So what happened? I remember something about the cocktail drinks?"

"It makes sense now. It must have been those cocktails that we had. I figured you ordered them when you went to the bathroom," she said.

"No, I didn't. I thought that you had ordered them while you were waiting for me."

"I feel terrible, I should have said something."

"No, don't blame yourself; it's not your fault. We are going to have to be more careful from now on, at least for the next coming weeks, months maybe. And you don't feel sick at all? Have you been checked out by the doctors?"

"Yes, they did an examination and could quickly tell that I had not come into contact with the poison. They even took blood just to be safe. The results will be back with yours."

Gabby left the hospital to go home for a shower and take Daniel home for a bit and also to let Josh rest. Josh lay in the hospital bed, feeling paranoid, not knowing how he was going to ensure his safety and that of Gabby and Daniel as well. "What if Gabby had drunk it instead?" he thought. It gave him chills. If something happened to her, he would never be able to forgive himself.

The work was only just starting. This was new territory for him. He thought about all the people he was investigating and wondered if it could really be the work of Wikus Louw. He was considered a white collar criminal by the allegations against him, not a murderer! It would be an extremely risky move, trying to take somebody's life, especially amidst investigations against him. It didn't make sense to Josh. And also what didn't add up was that the poison was Chinese or Japanese related.

The poison could have probably been located anywhere, though; black markets were everywhere for this kind of stuff. If the person behind this was successful in killing him, the investigation would still carry on without him. Was he really the target, or was it someone out to get Rhonda Martins or Detective Sidd? Maybe someone was going to try pick them off one by one? His thoughts wondered from one possible scenario to another until he eventually fell asleep.

***

Josh faintly heard the hospital room door open. Was he dreaming? It was dark and the moonlight shining through the window's blinds wasn't enough for him to see. He could feel a presence in the room.

"Hello, nurse?" There was silence. Maybe he was dreaming or hallucinating because of all the medication. The doctor had said that the pain killers were strong. He was just being paranoid now; he needed to relax and rest.

But then he heard a footstep – there was definitely someone in his room. He reached behind his head for the nurse call button that he had placed under his pillow but was prevented from pushing it when he was grabbed by big, fat, pork-sausage-fingered hands attached to polony arms, which restrained his arms and were placed over his mouth before he could shout for help.

Two big bodies had snuck into his room, obviously to finish the job that the poison had failed to do. The thug on his right was holding his arm and blocking his mouth, the one on his left was holding his other arm and held both of his kicking legs, which hadn't reached one of his targets yet. He felt completely restrained, unable to move an inch. He attempted to scream but all that could be heard were muffled noises. One of them punched him in the stomach to make him stop screaming. The pain was immense and his body felt so fragile.

"Hurry up and finish him off. We need to get out of here," one of the men spoke, in a deep, gruff voice. Josh could smell both of them – sweat, alcohol and poor hygiene. The man blocking his mouth brought his thumb and forefinger together, pinching Josh's nose closed to prevent him from breathing. Josh struggled, helpless. He grabbed onto the large man's thick, hairy arms that felt like small tree trunks. He would be lifeless if he didn't escape quickly. The panic set in, his heart rate increased and the machines that he was hooked up to sounded an alarm. The thugs had not thought of the heart rate monitor connected to his chest.

"Shit! Someone is going to come in here. Leave him, it's too risky now." The door burst open and two nurses wheeled a cart into the room. The passage light outside the doorway shone brightly into Josh's room, half blinding him and exposing the two big men on either side of him.

The small nurse realised something was wrong. "Hey, excuse me, what are you doing? You can't be in here!"

Josh was still holding onto the one man's arms tightly, trying to free himself. With the light now shining into the room, Josh noticed that the man had a snake tattoo on the inside of his forearm. A snake slithering through the eye sockets of a human skull.

The thugs did not waste another second. They both sprinted for the door, making heavy thuds with every stride. Moving that much weight was a lot of effort, but they were surprisingly fast. They knocked the two nurses to the ground, crashing the cart over in the process. Josh saw only the backs of his untrained assassins leaving. He pushed the emergency alarm button, but it was too late.

Detective Sidd burst into the room moments later with his gun out. "What happened?" he asked.

"Two guys tried to finish me off. They ran that way." Josh tried to catch his breath and pointed in the direction of the escapees. Detective Sidd chased after them. Josh climbed out of bed and checked on the nurses. Both were okay, visibly shaken but with no injuries except a bump and a bruise each. He suddenly felt faint. The excitement and struggle had strained his body.

Half an hour later Detective Sidd returned to the room. "They got away. I managed to get plates, but my bet is that it belongs to a stolen vehicle. Are you okay?"

"Yeah, I'm alright. I didn't know it was this dangerous when I signed up for the job."

"Neither did we, which means that we are on the right track. We will beef up security. I have arranged to have police patrolling the hospital and for one to be stationed in the hallway at all times during your stay here. Rhonda will be here in a few minutes. I gave her a call about twenty minutes ago. She wants to see you. She feels terrible and so do I! She will also brief you on everything that we have uncovered so far and will explain the way forward. Did you manage to get a description of them at all?"

"No, it was dark. But I did see that one of them had a snake tattoo on the inside of his forearm," Josh said and described it to Detective Sidd.

When Rhonda Martins arrived she showed deep concern for Josh's well-being and apologised profusely about what was happening to him. She even offered him an out of the investigation with no consequences for breach of the agreement he signed if he wanted it, but asked that he at least sleep on it. No decisions needed to be made immediately.

"With the feedback from the doctor about the poison, we have reached out to our Asian intelligence agencies to request any information on possible persons of interest leaving their countries and entering ours. It's worth a shot. You never know where you will get lucky in an investigation. They have undertaken to get back to me in the next day or two. However, that particular poison could just as well have been purchased in the back alleys of the city. I've been informed that it's relatively common. At this stage we obviously can't link it to anyone despite any suspicions we may have," she said. Detective Sidd just nodded quietly.

She continued. "We are going to increase your security detail. I will arrange everything early tomorrow morning with my team and fill you in thereafter. We will need to have central places for the investigation to be performed. My preference would be your law firm office. It has great physical and cyber security that we will add to. We can set up an investigation station for you and Mark and then headquarters will be at the Ranch House for briefing sessions, which we will arrange timeously. For now, try get some rest, you're going to need your strength tomorrow."

Josh was wide awake now. It was only 8PM; that would explain Detective Sidd's almost perfect timing, stopping by at the end of visiting hours. Josh was afraid to fall asleep. The policeman standing guard in the hallway came in to introduce himself and assure Josh that nobody would get past him. Josh believed him. Josh asked the night nurse for a sedative and went straight to sleep.

CHAPTER NINE

Hospital

THE NEXT MORNING JOSH WOKE to Gabby reading a magazine, her feet resting on his bed.

"Josh, how are you feeling?" she asked. "Detective Sidd told me about last night. I didn't want to wake you. I took the day off. I can't believe this." She raced through everything with a panic in her voice.

"Hey, Gabs. Everything is fine now. Detective Sidd and Rhonda assured me that they have it all under control. Security is going to be increased and there is a plan for everyone's safety, especially you and Daniel. I'm sorry that you are around all of this, it must be so scary for you and Daniel. I had no idea it would turn to this."

They discussed the events of the night before, with Josh downplaying much of the severity of his life-threatening experience. Rhonda and Detective Sidd made an appearance around teatime, when the hospital was serving tea and biscuits.

They explained to Josh and Gabby that the prosecutor's office had received anonymous threats regarding its investigation into the books and corporate affairs of Hillstrong Holdings. They had briefed their security team and there would be police patrolling

Josh and Gabby's neighbourhood. They advised that when Josh was discharged from the hospital it would be in the best interests of everyone if they stayed close to one another, and recommended that they even stayed together for a while.

Josh and Gabby gave each other a quick glance at the thought of living with each other. Obviously Josh had thought about it often, just under different circumstances. He wondered whether Gabby had considered it. They were each given a list of numbers to phone for emergencies that were programmed into their phones on speed dial.

Although there were no suspects at the moment, the threats seemed to be amateurish and not well thought out, which would explain the clumsy night job. Rhonda explained the timeline for the investigation and the plans for continuing to review all the files as soon as possible. Josh would be ready to resume work in a couple of days provided he didn't take the "out" that Rhonda had offered him. The idea was to conclude the investigation as soon as possible, but within twelve months from the date of opening the investigation. That would give them until just before Christmas.

***

Shirley stopped by the hospital with a basketful of nuts and biltong, and Josh's favourite motorsport and business magazines. She hugged Josh with tears in her eyes which made smudges on her pink reading glasses, hugging him like a mother would. She reassured Josh that she would have everything under control at the office. He told her to take two weeks off, get away from the office and have a long overdue holiday. Now that he didn't have many ongoing matters he didn't need her to be sitting manning the phones. She could divert all calls to her cell phone and just send him email updates when necessary.

The doctor did rounds and checked the results of the blood tests performed for Josh as well as Gabby. They were right with their first assessment: Gabby's blood stream was clear of the poison and Josh's was improving well. Things were looking better. Josh would spend one more night at the hospital and then he would be allowed to go home on condition that he did not over-exert himself. Gabby assured the doctor that she would be staying with Josh and would make sure he rested and had somebody at his side at all times.

That answered Josh's question about whether she would stay with him. To his surprise, she had not even bothered asking him what he thought about it. He liked a woman who was assertive at times. She would bring some of hers and Daniel's clothes over and they would stay in the spare room.

Josh's parents arrived as Gabby was saying goodbye; she had a full day showing clients houses. She kissed him on the mouth and held onto him tightly. Elizabeth Carter embraced her affectionately as one who was part of the family. She thanked her for everything that she had done for Josh and commented that she was so happy to see them together.

Something was bothering his parents, but Josh couldn't quite place his concern. They could possibly just be upset about what had happened to him, but he sensed an underlying problem and his gut was usually correct about these things, especially when it came to his parents. He could ask his mother anything, so he waited until his father offered to go buy coffee for himself and his mother at the hospital café before he enquired about his suspicion.

"Mom, is something wrong? Other than me lying in this hospital bed."

"It's nothing you need to worry yourself about at the moment. Just concentrate on getting better, Joshy," she said.

"Mom," said Josh. and gave her a look that showed he was obviously going to concern himself with anything that troubled his mother.

"It's just that your father and I have taken a big hit on our retirement savings from the Hillstrong Holdings crash," she said. Josh could hear the emotion in her voice rising up. It was obviously causing her a great deal of stress.

"How much did you lose?"

"Almost all of it, Joshy. About ninety percent of it," she said, now with tears in her eyes.

"Ninety percent! Mom! How did that happen? Why was there so much invested in Hillstrong? Surely your investment broker would have advised you to diversify your investments!" He was angry at the thought of them making such a foolish decision after he had gone to all the effort of helping his parents with investment advice a while ago.

"That's the thing, Joshy. We don't remember ever doing it. Especially after you sat with us and discussed the best investment strategies, we would never have put all our eggs in one basket. But the investment broker has all the forms with your father's signature authorising him to do it."

That didn't sound right to Josh either. No reputable investment broker would make such a decision with a person's retirement funds. Maybe a young investor looking for higher reward would be willing to take a higher risk, but not pensioners.

"Your dad will speak to you about it once he has made sure he understands all the implications. He has been beyond stressed about it too; he just doesn't show it. You know how your father is."

"Yeah, I know, Mom. I'll look into it," he said as his father walked back in with two coffees. Josh's mother squeezed his hand to say thank you and wiped her tears away.

"One cappuccino at your service, darling," said Alan Carter to his wife. Josh was used to the way that his parents treated each other, but now that he and Gabby had drawn closer and he could see a future with her and Daniel his parents' relationship really stood out to him.

Josh and his father went through the motorsport magazine, commenting on cars and performance parts they liked, and spoke mostly about the upcoming race his father would be taking part in for the BMW Racing Club at Kyalami racetrack. They discussed car setup and race tactics for the event. As much as he was enjoying the company, Josh was battling to stay awake. His mother could see this and insisted his father leave him so that their son could get some rest.

Josh slept for most of the day, woken only by the nurses checking his drip and offering him food and tea at meal times. He wasn't used to doing nothing all day, he felt useless, but it was just what he needed because of the physical exhaustion that his body was experiencing.

Night time came and Gabby and Daniel stopped by for another visit. Daniel sat on Josh's bed and showed him his latest card pack that gave descriptions of the engine specifications of supercars. He made Josh guess which car was on the back of the card by reading out the engine specs. Daniel was amazed that Josh didn't get one wrong. What Daniel didn't realise, because he hadn't started reading properly yet, was that the car was named on the back of the card. Gabby caught on very quickly and smiled at the boys and their games.

Daniel said he would look for a pack of cards that had bikes on them and maybe it would be more of a challenge for Josh. Josh accepted this challenge happily.

Gabby shared the news that she had a prospective buyer for two of her houses and was sure that she would sell them by the end of the week. Josh dozed off many times during conversations.

***

Wikus Louw was sitting in his lounge on his lavish leather couch watching the fire crackling while swirling a glass of whiskey on the rocks, his sixth glass for the evening. He stared around the room where most of his belongings had been seized by the operation run by that prosecuting bitch and that lawyer. He was listening to the news in the background covering the investigation and all the accusations and rumours that were surfacing, some completely false, mere gossip to sell magazines, and others unfortunately true. Of course, he would deny everything regardless of the accuracy.

Somehow, despite his extremely sensitive and subtle manner in handling his personal affairs, either the financial records or possibly paperwork that was seized had revealed that he had purchased his alleged mistress a multi-million Rand sea-view apartment and a sports car. His wife wasn't talking to him anyway, since he hadn't sounded convincing enough about his innocence regarding the alleged fraud committed. He supposed she would just add the affair to the list as well. The truth was that she hadn't known about any of it, and what she heard on the news and read in the newspapers was just the tip of the ice-berg.

His life was crumbling beneath him. The fall had been great, from revered billionaire and admired businessman to fraudster and adulterer. What would his kids say? All his neighbours and business associates who'd trusted him with his advice to invest as much of their money as possible in Hillstrong Holdings? So many lives were ruined, but they could hardly complain. "I made people rich over all these years," he thought. "They should be grateful they even had a taste of the good life. If it wasn't for me they all would have been mediocre businessmen, living mediocre lives."

There was a knock at the door. It had to be Willem, his only trusted associate left, and although not the sharpest cutlery in the kitchen drawer at least he was as loyal as a dog. He was the only person who hadn't run for the hills when the "accounting irregularities" were publicly announced, and he was also the only person who knew exactly where he was hiding out these days. Because he hadn't left the house in weeks, everyone in the neighbourhood and press had started speculating about him hiding away on his farm or even travelling abroad to some lavish location.

Willem entered the room and sat down opposite him on the couches by the fireplace. "The guys couldn't finish the job," Willem said, wary about what his boss would say towards his incompetence. Wikus Louw did not overact with anger and throw objects and curse words at him as Willem had expected him to do. That was certainly what would have happened a few months ago. A verbal berating from Wikus was as humiliating as anything he had ever experienced. But, since the news had broken, he seemed to have been brought down to everyone else's level. He seemed somewhat defeated in his attempts to regain control of his spiralling life. Besides, Willem was his only friend left and he still had use for him.

"Just keep trying until the job is done, but be discreet and only use people who you can trust. I can't risk the consequences of anything like this being traced back to me," Wikus said quietly. "And pour yourself a whiskey."

CHAPTER TEN

Discharged

WHEN HE COULD BE DISCHARGED, Gabby and Daniel arrived at the hospital to fetch Josh. They walked into the room just as Josh was attempting to dress himself. Daniel greeted him excitedly. The moment she walked in, Josh noticed that Gabby, however, was irritated about something and that her mood was different.

"Wait, let me help you with that," Gabby snapped. "Where are the nurses? You shouldn't be doing this yourself." She grabbed his shirt to put over his head. She didn't kiss him hello like she usually did.

She smells so good, Josh thought, but was distracted by her irritated mood. He wondered whether a house deal had fallen through.

"I am still able to dress myself, you know. I don't need the nurses for that," he said.

Gabby ignored his protests and spoke to him while helping him put on the rest of his clothes under the blanket. "I have packed a suitcase for Daniel and me. It's in the boot of my car. Vee phoned me and asked me to stop by Isabelle's on my way in this morning, so I did that quickly. She has given us meals for the next few days, for all three of us – " Gabby stopped mid-sentence as if she decided not to finish it, but then continued " – and she gave me your suit jacket that you left at her place."

Well, that was it. He could hear it in her tone when she said, "you left at her place". Josh couldn't remember when that must have been but it must have been a long time ago.

"Gabs –" he began, but she quickly started speaking over him. "I'm going to the front desk to complete the discharge forms for you. There is a two-man officer escort that is going to follow us home. Detective Sidd asked his men to inform him when you are on your way so that he can meet you at home and quickly update you on a few things."

"Sounds like you have everything covered, nurse-detective-investigator Gabby," Josh said, trying to lighten the mood. She gave a feeble attempt at a smile and left the room. That was a poor judgement call on Vee's side, he thought to himself. She could have given the suit to me many times before or even waited until I saw her again.

**

They left the hospital and were followed by the police escort. Waiting in his driveway for him was Detective Sidd. He greeted them and helped carry in all the bags and food from the car.

"I am not going to take up too much of your time, Josh. It's important that you rest. I just want to update you on the procedure of the investigation going forward. Given our recent events we will have to be extremely secure and discreet. This afternoon our team will attend at your firm's office to set up a secure network. This is for us to access the investigation's evidence comprising the forensic photographs and documents.

"Don't feel pressured to start too soon, but we also can't afford to waste any time. Take a few days to rest and then we will get started. We have been afforded printing rights for any photographs and documents. We will be installing filing cabinets that are electronically locked and connected to the network so we can track the access thereto and be alerted in the event that anyone unauthorised accesses any evidence.

"There will also be two large lock boxes for all the important evidence items such as memory cards, and other objects that were seized. Just inform the team where you want everything set up and they will do the rest. They are very professional, they know what they are doing and they won't make a mess either, so don't worry about that. They are also to perform a sweep of the office to make sure that you haven't been bugged at any time. At the moment we are considering all possibilities.

"Rhonda and I had a discussion that, since Gabby will be around a lot, she will be exposed to the evidence and investigation in due course. We feel confident that we can rely on her discretion. However, protocol is that she signs the non – disclosure and confidentiality document as well. I have a copy here to leave with you."

Gabby smiled and nodded in agreement. "I'll have my lawyer look over it." She gestured towards Josh and they all laughed. She can't be too mad then, Josh thought. Laughing hurt like hell for Josh. He clutched his stomach and bent over. Gabby immediately attended to Josh to support him standing.

"You must go lie down now," she said. "The doctor made it clear to me that you have to rest as much as possible."

"Alright. I must be off. Be sure to get some rest, Josh. If you need anything, you have my number. We have set up regular patrol vehicles around the clock. I will be interested in your views on the evidence when you get the chance. Start with the search and seizure report; it makes for an interesting read! Otherwise, I'll see you at the Ranch House in a week or so for the next briefing. You can bring Gabby and the kid too, stay the night and make a mini holiday out of it. There are plenty of rooms and we have the staff on call for game drives too. I'm considering bringing my wife and daughter as well. I'll be in touch." He wished them well and left.

"I want to go to the Rarnsh House," Daniel said.

Gabby tousled his hair. "We can talk about it later. Go play PlayStation so long while I get Josh settled in."

Daniel didn't need a second invitation. He went straight to the PlayStation and put on his favourite racing game. Josh lay down while Gabby unpacked the bags and took some food out for them for lunch. He slept for a few hours while Gabby and Daniel sat out by the pool. He woke up and walked to the kitchen. Every step made his stomach muscles tense and ache with pain. He opened the fridge and noticed that she'd even gone to the grocery store and picked out some of his favourite foods and snacks. She knew him scarily well. The place felt so homey with her and Daniel around. Josh knew that this was how he wanted to spend his days, with Gabby and Daniel, all the time, together as a family.

By that night, Josh had informed the investigation team that the secure network could be connected to his firm's server and the filing cabinets set up in the large boardroom – they could make that the War Room for the investigation. He gave them a set of access codes. His firm had high tech security; he had made sure of it, considering he stored highly confidential information. He called Shirley and told her what was happening so that she could expect the changes to the office when she got back to work. She would also receive the electronic passwords to the cabinets and server as she would be assisting with the printing and filing of the evidence.

When Daniel was asleep, Josh walked to the TV room where Gabby was sitting. They hadn't addressed the issue about his suit jacket being at Vee's place yet. Gabby seemed to be ignoring it for fear of hearing something she did not want to and Josh did not feel like having this type of conversation with her. It were as if they were both ignoring it. However, it wasn't resolved and so was always lingering under the surface of every conversation. She hadn't looked him in the eye since she'd been given the jacket. He felt nervous to talk to her about it. He would much rather face a judge and be under cross examination himself than with Gabby. This was the first time he'd ever felt this way.

"Gabs, can we talk?" he said.

"Sure," she said coldly, without looking at him. She was hurt.

"About my jacket at Vee's place," he started, thinking how best to phrase it. "It's from a long time ago, before I met you," he said.

Gabby finally looked at him. "How long ago? You never told me that the two of you ever had anything between you."

"I spent the night at Isabelle's because I had had too much to drink. It was only one time. We never even dated or anything. I'm sorry I didn't tell you. It just didn't come up and it didn't mean anything to me. Vee and I are just friends and nothing more," he said.

"Josh, if you're not ready for a family I need to know. I can't go through what I've been through again. I've had my share of womanisers and I won't do it again. It's also not fair on Daniel either. He really looks up to you and if you're not in this then we need to know," she said firmly, a tear running down her cheek. "I need to know whether I made a mistake letting you in."

Josh got painfully up from his chair and sat next to Gabby on the couch. He took her hands in his. "Gabs, I'm all in, I promise. You have nothing to worry about with me. I'm not like the men in your past!"

"I know that. It's just that it caught me off guard. I got worried because we haven't exactly spoken about us and I thought that perhaps you saw us as not being exclusive."

"Gabs, we are exclusive, I promise!"

She relaxed. Josh could see the weight lifted off her shoulders. It had been an extremely emotional and stressful few days. She cuddled up next to Josh and they sat in silence for a while. He was glad that the cross examination had been brief.

***

Over the next week Josh hardly worked at all. He spent his days resting at home, watching TV, and found himself waiting for Gabby to get home between showing houses and fetching Daniel from school. He was getting used to the idea of them being home with him and felt a tinge of loneliness as soon as they left. How the bachelor life had changed so suddenly, but so easily at the same time.

He was feeling stronger by the day too. He was more active by the eighth day and the three of them took casual walks around the neighbourhood in the early evenings before dinner to get him out of the house and loosen up his muscles. By the second week he was taking a slow jog in the morning, feeling quite confident that his strength had almost returned and the last trace of poison had worked itself out of his body. He had just finished his last course of medication and was ready to get back to work.

On the Sunday evening before returning to the Ranch House he sat at his home office desk and went through the search and seizure reports. The operation conducted at Hillstrong Holdings revealed almost nothing helpful. The only thing that stood out was the lack of evidence, which in itself portrayed a suspicious activity that all documents were either destroyed or removed off-site.

The operation at the home of Wikus Louw with Detective Sidd was a different story. He looked at the photographs annexed to the report and was amazed at the mansion. He now realised the kind of wealth that he was dealing with: the artwork, furniture and sheer size of the residence. He looked at all of the photographs of the evidence and made notes of all the items of interest that caught his attention and that he would be following up on. Most of it was the contents of the home office of Wikus Louw, the conference phone memory card, other storage devices found in the walk-in safe, and the files of documents stashed away in the safe.

Most peculiar was the oil canvass of Napoleon Bonaparte, which Josh thought spoke of the high opinion that Wikus must have of himself. And then there were the ornaments placed on the desk. He looked particularly at the koi ornament and felt like he had seen that before, but couldn't quite place it. He made his notes and found himself more and more excited about the investigation. He loved his job. This is what he was born to do. Perhaps over time his legal practice would develop into special legal investigations.

CHAPTER ELEVEN

Ranch House

JOSH WAS BACK AT THE Ranch House for his second briefing session, Gabby was attending her first, and much to Daniel's disappointment, he was at preschool. Gabby had promised that he could attend the Ranch House next time, wanting to see what it was like before taking her child with her. Already the guards at the gates made her nervous. Detective Sidd had also phoned Josh to say that his wife and daughter wouldn't be attending this time either.

They went through the routine car search and made their way to the investigation headquarters. Her expression was the same as Josh's when he had seen the Ranch House for the first time – sheer amazement.

Inside, Detective Sidd and Rhonda drank coffee and chatted until the rest of the team arrived. They greeted Josh and Gabby warmly, Rhonda and Gabby even hugged hello. They had sparked a friendship during the last two weeks by staying in contact more than just for the investigation. This made Josh happy, knowing that Gabby was comfortable in his world and making a good impression. They had lunch outside on the balcony overlooking the river while watching animals in small groups make their way to the watering hole. The food that was served was a gourmet meal that could be expected at a five star restaurant in the city. After lunch they made their way to the conference room and received a first-hand account from Detective Sidd of the events of the search and seizure at the home of Wikus Louw.

Rhonda then began the feedback from the prosecutor's office. "The investigation team back at my office are busy reviewing the evidence that was collected and what is apparent is that this investigation appears to be going in the exact same direction as the internationally famous Enron scandal. Today, I think it is important just to go over that case and highlight the similarities of what we are dealing with to assist with our investigation, not to close off any other avenues. At the very least, it will educate us on what to look for in a matter of this large a scale.

"South Africa will be making history with this investigation because of the global reach and drastic consequences that have been felt thus far and what is still to come, and so I want to make sure we create a precedent for the rest of the world to follow." Everyone nodded in agreement.

She continued. "The files taken from the safe behind the bookcase in Wikus Louw's home office, which our skilled detective here so expertly uncovered," she pointed at Detective Sidd, who raised his hand in appreciation of the acknowledgement, "comprised at least twenty merger matters that highlight the group's structural strategies in relation to its accounting practices and how they have been able to improve their financial position year after year at an astronomical rate.

"As was the case with Enron and other scandal-ridden corporations over the years, Hillstrong Holdings has appeared to comply with all legal and regulatory requirements in its various jurisdictions. This has created a false sense of security and trust from both investors and other stakeholders.

"Josh, I know you are very well acquainted with the Enron matter. Would you be so kind as to talk us through it?"

Josh had once done an entire five-page exposé in the Business Times unpacking the dangers of ineffective legal and regulatory standards for public companies. The article, as well as his many courtroom victories, led to him being nominated for the "Corporate Attorney of the Year" award a few years before. He'd won that award and grew his client base threefold as a result of the exposure.

"Yes, sure." Josh confidently stood and walked to the front of the conference room to make eye contact with the rest of the team, and Gabby. Even though the conference room boasted an incredible view of nature through the large glass doors, Gabby's eyes were fixed on him.

"Enron Corporation was an American energy, commodities and services company based in Houston, Texas. It was founded in 1985 as a merger between two relatively small regional companies, Houston Natural Gas and InterNorth. The story of Enron is the story of a company that reached incredible heights, only to face a horrific fall. Already you can see where I am going with this; the share price of Hillstrong Holdings fell off a cliff in a matter of days after news spread of the accounting irregularities.

"Enron's collapse affected thousands of employees and shook Wall Street to its core. At Enron's peak, its shares were worth $90.75. When it declared bankruptcy in December 2001, they were trading at $0.26. To this day, many wonder how such a powerful business, at the time one of the largest companies in the U. S, disintegrated almost overnight and how it managed to fool the regulators with fake holdings and off – the-books accounting for so long.

"In comparison, Hillstrong Holdings highest share price was R96 and has fallen to a share price of R1.40, a loss in the hundreds of billions for the South African economy, banks and investors and retirees, as well as international companies that had invested with Hillstrong. We will have to conclude our due diligence on the group structure and determine whether similar off-the-books companies were used by Hillstrong to inflate its profits and hide debts so that its balance sheet reflected growth and profits at an extremely impressive rate.

"Back to Enron. Following the merger, the CEO Kenneth Lay re-branded Enron into an energy trader and supplier. Deregulation of the energy markets meant that the energy sector was being transferred from government control into a free market system and allowed companies to place bets on future prices, and Enron was in a position to take advantage of that. Enron would purchase electricity from different entities and supply it to individual users. In 1990, Lay created the Enron Finance Corporation. To manage it, he appointed Jeffrey Skilling, whose accounting abilities had made him one of the youngest partners at his previous auditing firm.

"Skilling joined Enron at a very opportune time, when the regulatory environment allowed Enron to grow exponentially. At the end of the 1990s, internet stocks comprising the dot-com bubble were being valued at unthinkable levels and, as a result, most investors and regulators merely accepted spiking share prices as the new normal.

"One of Skilling's early decisions was to change Enron's accounting methods from a traditional historical cost accounting method to a mark-to-market accounting method, for which the company got official SEC approval in 1992. This means that a measurement of the fair value of accounts, meaning assets and liabilities, can change over time. Mark- to-market aims to provide a realistic valuation of a company's current financial position. It is a legitimate and widely-used practice. However, in some cases it can be manipulated, because this method of accounting is not based on 'actual' cost but on 'fair value', which is harder to put a value to. Some believe this accounting method was where Enron's troubles began, as it essentially started logging estimated profits as actual profits.

"In 1999, Enron created Enron Online, an electronic trading website that focused on commodities. Enron was the counter-party to every one of its online transactions. It was either the buyer or the seller. To attract participants and trading partners, Enron presented its reputation, credit and expertise in the energy sector as trust in the market. Enron was praised for its expansions and ambitious projects, and was named 'America's Most Innovative Company' by Fortune Magazine for all the years between 1996 and 2001.

"This sounds familiar, again because of Hillstrong Holdings' reputation for its exponential growth and returns for its investors throughout all the years, until now, of course. Wikus Louw was praised as an entrepreneurial genius and deal-maker of the year for multiple years in a row.

"In 2000, Enron entered into a partnership with the dominating video rental chain, Blockbuster. Entering into the video market was a very obvious move to make, but with the accounting method adopted by Enron it started logging expected earnings based on expected growth of the video market, which vastly inflated the numbers. Not even six months had passed when Enron Online was executing nearly $350 billion in trades.

"When the dot-com bubble began to burst, Enron thought it could take advantage of it by building high-speed broadband telecommunication networks. Hundreds of millions of dollars were spent on this project, but the company ended up realising almost no profit. Then came the recession. A few months after that and Enron was caught with its pants down, being exposed to the most volatile parts of the market. As a result, many trusting investors and creditors found themselves on the losing end of a vanishing market cap.

"By the end of the year 2000, Enron was falling apart, but thanks to the mark-to-market accounting method the CEO and financial head had a way of hiding the financial losses of the trading business and other operations of the company, essentially using this technique to measure the value of a share based on its current market value, instead of its book value. This can work well when trading shares, but it can be fatal for actual businesses.

"To give you a practical example, let's say for argument's sake the company builds an asset, such as an energy power plant, and immediately claims the projected profit on its books, even though it hasn't made any profit from it. If eventually the revenue from the power plant is less than the projected amount that it has entered in its books earlier, then, instead of writing up the loss in the company's books, it will transfer the asset to an off-the-books corporation, where the loss would go unreported.

"This type of accounting enabled Enron to write off unprofitable activities without hurting its bottom line. So its balance sheet always looked impeccable. It did not, however, have the assets and revenue to back up what the financial statements were showing investors and shareholders.

"Clearly, you can see that the mark-to-market accounting practice led to schemes that were designed to hide the losses and make the company appear to be more profitable than it really was. To survive with the mounting liabilities, Andrew Fastow, an accountant who was promoted to CFO in 1998, came up with a deliberate plan to make the company appear to be in sound financial shape, despite the fact that many of its subsidiaries were losing money.

"Let's look at how Enron managed to hide all of its debt. The CFO and others at Enron came up with a plan to use off-balance-sheet entities called special purpose vehicles to hide its debt and poor performing or loss-making assets from investors and creditors. The primary aim of these entities was to hide accounting realities, rather than operating results. They did this by effectively buying Enron's debt from it.

"The standard transaction involving Enron and a special purpose vehicle would go something like this: Enron would transfer some of its rapidly rising stock to the entity in exchange for cash or a credit note. The off-the-book entity would then use the stock to hedge an asset listed on Enron's balance sheet. In turn, Enron would guarantee the entity's value to reduce apparent counter-party risk.

"These entities themselves were not illegal, even though their sole purpose was to hide accounting realities. They were different from standard debt securitisation in several ways. One major difference was that the entities were capitalised entirely with Enron stock. This directly compromised the ability of the entity to hedge if Enron's share prices fell.

"Just as dangerous was the second significant difference: Enron's failure to disclose conflicts of interest. Enron disclosed the entities' existence to the investing public, although it's certainly likely that few people understood them, but it failed to adequately disclose the non-arm's length deals between the company and the entities.

"If we dig into the Hillstrong Holdings historical financial accounts and its SENS announcements in respect of the Johannesburg Stock Exchange alone, it is doubtful that Hillstrong disclosed its off-the-books entities at all and, if it did, the group structures would also be too complex for the average investor to understand.

"Enron, its shareholders and investors, just like Hillstrong, all believed that its stock price would keep rising, before its collapse in 1998. Eventually, Enron's stock declined and the values of the entities also fell, forcing Enron's guarantees to take effect. Similarly, Hillstrong had billions of Rand of loans from banks backed with their own stock as security. All the guarantees and cessions and pledges were called in the moment the share price was less than the cover for the loans.

"In addition to the CFO, a major player in the Enron scandal was Enron's accounting firm, Arthur Andersen, and the partner David Duncan, who oversaw Enron's accounts. As one of the five largest accounting firms in the United States at the time, Andersen had a reputation for high standards and quality risk management. However, despite Enron's poor accounting practices, Arthur Andersen offered its stamp of approval, signing off on the corporate reports for years – which was enough for investors and regulators.

"However, this game couldn't go on forever. By April 2001, many analysts started to question Enron's earnings and their transparency. The exact same situation has happened with Hillstrong. It is highly questionable why the auditing firms have signed off the financials year after year, only to suddenly not sign off the financial statements for reasons of accounting irregularities, especially when they are also going to restate the financial statements for the past years."

Gabby sat in the conference chair, mesmerised by Josh's ability to take such a complex story and explain it in a manner that even she, who was someone who didn't really take an interest in corporate fraud or corporate anything, could follow and find interesting.

"By 2001, Enron's share price plummeted. The CEO retired earlier that year, offering the position to the CFO and then, later that year, the CFO also resigned for 'personal reasons'. Analysts downgraded Enron's share price rating and the stock price dropped even further. The company started closing down entities because of the losses so that it wouldn't have to distribute shares which would have the effect of reducing the value of the stock even more. But this mistake attracted the attention of the Securities and Exchange Commission – the SEC – which is the equivalent to South Africa's Financial Services Board – FSB.

"Enron, in an attempt not to go bankrupt, then decided to change pension plan administrators, which forbade employees from selling their shares for at least thirty days. Shortly thereafter, the SEC announced it was investigating Enron and the off-the-book entities created by it. Also, the company restated earnings going back to 1997. The result was that Enron had losses of $591 million and had $628 million in debt by the end of 2000.

"The final blow was dealt when a company that had previously announced it would merge with Enron backed out of the deal later that year. This caused Enron to file for bankruptcy by the end of that year. Once Enron's Plan of Reorganization was approved by the United States Bankruptcy Court, the new board of directors changed Enron's name to Enron Creditors Recovery Corp. The company's new sole mission was 'to reorganise and liquidate certain of the operations and assets of the "pre-bankruptcy" Enron for the benefit of creditors'.

"There have been rumours that Hillstrong Holdings' related entities are preparing papers to apply to court for the scheme of arrangement and agreement with creditors to prevent a fire sale of their assets. A scheme of arrangement would be the Hillstrong-related entities only chance to realise as close to the real face value of their assets as possible.

"Is everyone following me so far?" Josh asked the room and everyone nodded, including Gabby. Rhonda was right up there with Josh and Detective Sidd wasn't far off, although he was no commercially-minded cop. His speciality was investigating and finding criminals. Short and sweet.

Josh continued. "The next part is going to be a preview of where we are heading with our case – meaning the end goal of our investigation will be to hold accountable everyone who was part of this corporate fraud. The obvious answer is Wikus Louw, but we must determine which of his associates are involved too. Anybody who was involved in unregulated dealings or unlawful activities.

"In the Enron story, the auditing firm – Arthur Andersen – was one of the first casualties of Enron's prolific demise. In June 2002, the firm was found guilty of obstructing justice for shredding Enron's financial documents to conceal them from the SEC. Due to the lack of evidence found at the Hillstrong offices during our search and seizure operation, I fear that Hillstrong Holdings employees may have done the same. At the very least they have stored the documents in an undisclosed location, which would essentially be the same as obstructing justice. However, if we find the documents we would be in a much better position than the investigation team on the Enron case.

"Several of Enron's executives were charged with a whole host of charges, including conspiracy, insider trading and securities fraud. The executives cashed out all of their stock before the share price dropped; they made millions while most people lost everything. I'm guessing that in our research, we will find that the executives of Hillstrong have benefited immensely despite the crash of the share price. We will have to perform background and lifestyle audits, although that won't be so clear as most of these individuals were extremely wealthy to begin with. Offshore vehicles of wealth and family trusts will be where the profits are stored.

"Anyone with shares at this moment is in a bad place so we are looking for the senior employees of Hillstrong who seem not to have taken a huge hit and also do not currently hold shares in Hillstrong in their personal capacities or related entities. We will then immediately look at the transactions to see when those shares were disposed of. Similarly to Enron, Wikus Louw hired employees of Hillstrong who were young, ambitious, loyal and money hungry. The type of people who could get the job done without asking too many questions and who would also turn a blind eye when those questions would arise.

"You might ask what the consequences are for Wikus Louw and his associates should they be found guilty. Well, for some perspective, Enron's founder and former CEO was convicted of six counts of fraud and conspiracy and four counts of bank fraud. In 2006, Skilling was convicted of conspiracy, fraud and insider trading. Skilling originally received a twenty-four-year sentence.

"At the time, Enron's collapse was the biggest corporate bankruptcy to ever hit the financial world, but since then the failures of WorldCom, Lehman Brothers and Washington Mutual have surpassed it. I think we are looking at gaining a lot of attention in the same pool of failed corporations."

Josh finished his part and the team discussed the most important avenues to pursue. Detective Sidd and Josh would work from the offices of Carter & Associates, Rhonda would work with her team at the prosecutor's offices. Everyone was warned to watch out for any suspicious activity at the office and keep a wary eye at home as well. Any disturbance or unusual behaviour by anyone around them should not be taken too lightly.

Gabby and Josh left the Ranch House and for the couple of hours' drive home they chatted away. Gabby seemed to be so alive and full of energy, she was so excited to be a part of this investigation with Josh. She reached over and held his hand as they drove to fetch Daniel from her parents' house.

CHAPTER TWELVE

The Legend of the Koi

Josh and Detective Sidd were at the offices of Carter & Associates, reviewing the cabinets of evidence still to be paged through and analysed. Josh was busy with email correspondence that had been deleted from Wikus Louw's computer, but which the IT technicians had been able to restore from the footprints of the files left behind. When dealing with electronic footprints, nothing was ever deleted forever; there would always be a trace.

A chain of emails caught Josh's attention, perhaps because of the name, at first, and then the context. The emails were from a Mr Simon Chen from China, the assistant of Mr Fei Hung, a Chinese business tycoon worth billions. The emails read as follows:

Dear Mr Louw,

Mr Hung was most pleased to meet you at the Sandton Convention Centre in South Africa last week. He proposes that the transaction proceeds on the basis that a financial, legal and business due diligence be performed into the business of Hillstrong Holdings. The confidentiality and non-

disclosure agreement has been signed by Mr Hung and is enclosed hereto for your counter signature.

I would like to take this opportunity to assure you and your staff that when Mr Hung commits to a transaction of this nature with such a substantial amount, Mr Hung will not spare any resources for the success of the business going forward. He sees a great opportunity for the merger to take primary market position globally.

We look forward to receiving the access to the due diligence documents of Hillstrong Holdings by close of business tomorrow, as discussed.

Yours faithfully, Simon Chen

Personal Advisor and Assistant to Mr Fei Hung

Josh followed the email chain to get to the reply from Wikus Louw:

Dear Mr Chen and Mr Hung,

Firstly, let me extend my gratitude for the gift that you presented me at the conclusion of our meeting. I will cherish this ornament along with all of my most esteemed business achievements as I view this opportunity with Hung Industries a huge achievement in itself.

Please find enclosed my countersigned confidentiality and non-disclosure agreement.

I confirm that my team will have the due diligence access available by close of business tomorrow for your team to begin their review of our files.

Yours sincerely, Wikus Louw

Josh spoke to himself loudly. "That is very interesting. He makes reference to an ornament, and I wonder if that could be what we found at his home?" He continued to read the email exchanges which were over the course of a few weeks.

"What you say, Josh?" asked Detective Sidd.

"Just hold on, I think I have found something," Josh answered and continued to read the emails.

Dear Mr Louw,

It is a great pleasure to have presented you with our gift. It is a token of our gratitude for your hospitality and our admiration for your achievements in the business world. In our culture, the parable of the koi and the dragon is the ultimate achievement and we consider our business venture something that will lead us there.

Yours faithfully, Simon Chen

Personal Advisor and Assistant to Mr Fei Hung

"Of course! How could I forget? I knew that koi ornament had a meaning behind it! I read the myth years ago when I was researching and starting my hobby of my Japanese garden at home. There are so many myths and legends in the Japanese and Chinese culture. I came across the legend when I was installing a mini waterfall and buying fish for my pond. There is a cultural blog that tells the story," Josh said as he looked for the blog that he had once come across that revealed the symbolism. He found it easily as Chinese symbols and culture was a niche interest that one wouldn't easily stumble upon unless one was searching for that information. He read out the koi ornament's meaning to Detective Sidd:

"Koi are a legendary fish. Graceful, vibrant, and one of the most recognizable fish in the world, koi are well-loved and respected. Often associated with Japan, koi actually originated from Central Asia in China. They were introduced to Japan by Chinese invaders. The koi got their name around 500 BC, but the fish itself has been around for much longer. Fossils of ancient koi date back twenty million years. Natural genetic mutation brought about the brilliant colours in koi known today, and in the early 1800s Japanese farmers began keeping them for aesthetics. Over the years, koi fish meaning and symbolism has become iconic around the world.

"Where did I see that story? Oh, here we go – it's called the Waterfall Legend and goes as follows.

"One particular legend is the koi fish's claim to fame. An ancient tale tells of a huge school of golden koi swimming upstream the Yellow River in China. Gaining strength by fighting against the current, the school glimmered as they swam together through the river. When they reached a waterfall at the end of the river, many of the koi turned back, letting the flow of the river carry them away. The remaining koi refused to give up. Leaping from the depths of the river, they attempted to reach the top of the waterfall, to no avail.

"Their efforts caught the attention of local demons, who mocked their efforts and heightened the waterfall out of malice. After a hundred years of jumping, one koi finally reached the top of the waterfall. The gods recognized the koi for its perseverance and determination and turned it into a golden dragon, the image of power and strength." Josh continued reading the article.

"Symbolism and meaning. Koi fish are associated with positive imagery. Because of the dragon legend, they are known as symbols of strength and perseverance, as seen in their determinative struggle upstream. And because of the lone koi that made it to the top of the waterfall, they are also known as symbols of a destiny fulfilled. Resulting from its bravery in swimming upstream, the koi is often-times associated with Samurai warriors in Japan.

"The integrity and high sense of character koi are known for makes them a symbol of achievement and honour. The koi is known for its strength, individuality, character and perseverance. Koi fish are also symbolised according to their colouration. Gold koi symbolise prosperity and wellbeing in business."

Josh looked up from his computer at Detective Sidd. "I think Wikus Louw is our golden koi, or dragon now. How the mighty dragon has fallen from fame and accomplishment."

He sat staring at the photograph of the koi and suddenly felt sick with the realisation that he'd just made the connection. "Mark, the ornament is Japanese and Chinese related, the poison that was slipped into my drink was also of that origin. Do you think this is the link we were looking for?"

"Well, shit Josh, you're right. I definitely think it's worth following that lead. When things seem to be a coincidence, it generally isn't. We just need to find a way to tie it directly to Wikus Louw or Fei Hung. If it is Wikus behind the poison then we can have him charged with attempted murder in addition to his corporate crimes. Now we are playing a whole new ball game!" Detective Sidd seemed to get excited that attempted murder was added to the investigation that was his bread and butter. "Let's add that to the board and see if any other evidence leads us further down the rabbit hole."

Detective Sidd stood up and walked over to the two large whiteboards that they were using as a large mind map and information consolidator. He wrote down their latest discovery next to the photograph of the golden koi ornament and linked that to the networking event at which Josh was poisoned.

"I don't remember Hung Industries ever concluding a merger with Hillstrong Holdings, though. I wonder if the deal fell through," Josh stated and then he came across another email chain that answered his question. Approximately four weeks after the first correspondence, Mr Chen seemed to have written back to Wikus Louw, raising some concerns.

Dear Mr Louw,

We have concluded our preliminary due diligence investigation into the affairs of Hillstrong Holdings and it seems that there is certain documentation missing from the virtual data room. In many cases we do not see disclosure of certain financial transactions and, furthermore, your legal agreements for the large transactions concluded are not uploaded.

We are sure the incorrect or draft financials have been uploaded in error and it has been a mere oversight that the legal agreements were not uploaded as well.

We request that the relevant documentation be uploaded as soon as possible so that our due diligence of Hillstrong Holdings can be finalised.

Thanking you in advance,

Mr Simon Chen
Personal Advisor and Assistant to Mr Fei Hung

Dear Mr Chen and Mr Hung,

I have been advised that the financial statements that have been uploaded on the virtual data room are indeed the correct ones and have been signed off by our auditors. We are of the view that our financials may look incomplete to an outsider as our group structure is extremely complex and the intra-group accounting practices allowed in South Africa may be different to those in Japan and other international countries. We assure you that our auditors have perused and have satisfied themselves with our financial statements.

In respect of legal agreements, you may find this strange but many of our deals have been concluded on the back of verbal agreements between business partners. At certain times, to keep up with the exponential growth of Hillstrong Holdings we were unable to delay the process by the drafting of contracts before implementing the deals. We have, however, an internal legal firm that reviews all deals concluded and where necessary extensive legal agreements are drafted to accompany the deal structures. We have found that in every event, the agreements have become redundant due to absorbing the entities into our group structure.

I trust that you find this in order and that we may proceed with the merger between Hillstrong and Hung Industries.

Yours sincerely, Wikus Louw

Josh couldn't believe what he had uncovered. There, in black and white, was an admission by Wikus Louw that he was implementing deals without the proper legal agreements in place. How on earth had he been reporting to shareholders and satisfying regulatory requirements for such a large public entity as Hillstrong? And given the nature and value of the mergers that Hillstrong was involved in, there was no way a transaction would be implemented without any agreements. It was unheard of. There would be extensive warranties and details of the purchase consideration and payment terms.

And finally, weeks after the end of the last email chain, was the nail in the coffin for the relationship between Hung Industries and Hillstrong Holdings.

Dear Mr Louw,

It is with regret that Mr Fei Hung must withdraw from this transaction. Upon further due diligence with our colleagues in South Africa it has been decided that Hillstrong Holdings would not be a good fit for Hung Industries. The vision and core values that underpin Hung Industries are vastly different from that of your Company and Mr Hung will not jeopardise the reputation that he has achieved with his board over a transaction that he does not believe will be in the best interests of Hung Industries, notwithstanding the exponential financial returns that you have assured him of.

We thank you for the opportunity and wish you success on your future endeavours.

Yours faithfully, Simon Chen

Personal Advisor and Assistant to Mr Fei Hung

Detective Sidd was done for the night and left. Josh would have to find out more about Hung Industries, Mr Fei Hung, and his assistant Simon Chen. His research would focus on the failed transaction between the two entities and what exactly was uncovered by Hung Industries that made them suddenly decide against the transaction. He locked up the office and headed home.

Gabby was putting Daniel to bed, who didn't want to sleep because he was so excited about the next day, as Josh was taking him to the racetrack to watch Alan Carter race in the BMW Club Racing Series at Kyalami Racetrack.

CHAPTER THIRTEEN

A Day at the Races

THE SUN WASN'T EVEN UP yet when Josh heard his phone buzzing with the sound of his alarm. He couldn't hear any movement in the house. He decided to take a shower first, before going to make coffee and waking Daniel. Feeling much more awake after his shower, he dressed and made his way to the kitchen. Gabby was standing drinking coffee. Daniel was eating a slice of toast.

"Morning. I made some coffee and am forcing Daniel to eat something. Knowing how excited he is, he will forget to eat anything all day," said Gabby.

Josh looked at her, thinking how attractive she was as a mother, how watching her doing the simplest of things for Daniel was so appealing to him.

"Well, we are one and the same, then. I'd better have some toast as well before I get into trouble with your mother too," he said to Daniel and gave him a wink. Josh drank his coffee and sat at the table next to Daniel.

"Aww, Josh, where did you get that hat? It's awesome," Daniel exclaimed, looking at the new Valentino Rossi number 46 hat that

Josh was wearing. Both Josh and Daniel were proud Rossi fans in the MotoGP.

"You like it?" Josh asked.

"It's the coolest hat I've ever seen!" Daniel answered.

"Well, that's good, because I got you a matching one just like it!" Josh reached up into the kitchen cupboard where he had been hiding the hat from Daniel and placed it on Daniel's head. Daniel thanked Josh profusely and ran off to look at himself in the mirror in his bedroom.

"You spoil him," Gabby said, staring lovingly into Josh's eyes. He stared right back into hers. She walked over and kissed him gently on the lips, just as Daniel walked into the kitchen.

"Hey, could you two get a room? Gee whizz," he said, and they all shared a laugh.

Josh and Daniel climbed into the BMW and waved goodbye to Gabby.

"See you later, boys. Be good." She waved them off.

The sun was just coming up as they drove out onto the highway towards Kyalami Racetrack. It was going to be a wonderfully hot day at the races.

Daniel looked at Josh and asked, "Are you and my mom boyfriend and girlfriend?"

Josh wasn't prepared for this at all but answered, "Something like that, bud. Is that okay?"

"That would be the best thing ever!" Daniel put Josh's nerves at ease immediately. "She really likes you, you know. She is so much happier since she met you. She used to be sad a lot when I was a baby. Like all alone and sad, especially when my dad used to fight with her. I can still remember him shouting a lot. I didn't like that at all. I am really glad she met you. And me," he said.

What a mature boy of seven years old, Josh thought. "I like your mother very much too, bud. She makes me a happier person as well."

Daniel stared out of the window at the cars that they were passing. "Can we race someone?" he pleaded. Josh and Daniel would often-times find another petrol head on the road and pull up next to them and slowly accelerate to get their attention. It would instantly become a race. It wasn't difficult to egg someone on to race, especially on a race day when many spectators were on the road going to the track. It was something that Josh's father had done with him when he was younger and now Josh would sometimes do the same with Daniel.

"If you find someone, let me know," Josh said, also eagerly looking out.

They were ten minutes from the track when Josh spotted his victim, an Audi RS5. Josh wondered if it was the naturally aspirated 4.2 litre V8 or the new 2.9 litre twin turbo V6 that the latest model came out with. They would soon find out. Josh pulled up alongside the Audi and immediately caught the driver's attention, almost as if the driver had seen Josh's BMW lights in the rear view mirror and was waiting for the first move to be made.

"How fast is that car, Josh? Are we going to win?" Daniel asked eagerly as he realised what was about to happen.

"I'm sure we have a good chance," Josh said, a huge, boyish smile on his face. The BMW and Audi rook the off-ramp from the highway towards the racetrack. There was a main, double lane up ahead with a robot and both drivers were begging for a red light. They received what they asked for.

The two cars stood at the red light waiting for the change to green. Josh watched the lights to the side to see when they turned orange so that he could time the pull-off just right. The Audi would have an edge off the line as it was all-wheel-drive. It would be an even match, the road ahead with few cars would be what made the difference.

The lights to the side went orange. Josh told Daniel to hold on and get ready. Both drivers prepared their cars, the grunting from the Audi could be heard inside the BMW. The red light turned to green and the cars launched off the line. The tyres screeched, but were controlled by the traction control. The Audi was ahead immediately with its all-wheel-drive system, but the BMW had the power to close the gap. The Audi had half a car's length gap ahead when the BMW closed in. The speedometer in the BMW climbed from 0-100km/h in just over four seconds. The boys were pushed back into their seats as the horsepower of the BMW accelerated up next to the Audi with ease and started passing the Audi with screams of victory from Daniel. Josh also had a performance pack on his car which put it in a league of its own.

With the BMW being the clear winner, the driver of the Audi let down his window and complimented Josh on his car and driving, to which Josh reciprocated. Petrol heads. They arrived at the racetrack and found parking close to the pits.

Alan and Elizabeth Carter were sitting on their camping chairs next to the race car, all ready for the qualifying to take place in the next hour. Josh kissed his parents hello, as did Daniel, who had become very fond of them after spending much time with Josh and going to the races. His father was still such a big man, although Josh could see the effects of ageing slowly setting in.

They helped themselves to coffee in the flask, juice for Daniel, and bacon rolls which had been prepared by Josh's mom the night before. Josh and his father walked around the car and checked the tyre pressure, fuel and wheel nuts, while Elizabeth spoke to Daniel, asking him all about his school and asking after his mother.

"Is the setup all done?" Josh asked his father

"Yip, the car is ready. Wheel nuts checked, windscreen clean. The tyres… I wasn't sure what pressure to go with. The air is cool and these semi-slicks warm up pretty quick. Decided on 1.6 bar back and 1.8 bar front."

"Sounds good," said Josh. "What's the plan of action for qualifying?"

"I'm going to go out as soon as we can and get as many laps as possible. Get the tyres warmed up and, when most of the drivers come into the pits, I'll hopefully get a good two or so laps in for time."

"Great, I like that plan. How's work, Dad?"

"It's going to be my last six months before I retire. I can't believe it's time already," he said in disbelief and then went quiet. Josh could see that he was stressed, and he knew it was about the investments.

The race organiser walked past the pits shouting above the noise of all the race cars idling and revving in preparation of qualifying, telling everyone to "round up and head out to the start". Alan grabbed his race helmet and gloves and climbed inside the car. Josh helped strap him in the racing harness, closed the door and wished him luck. Josh, his mother and Daniel made their way to the rooftop grandstand where they had the best vantage point for the track. Alan, being the leader this season was more competitive this season than ever before.

Josh's mother took the quiet time to catch up with her son and find out about his work and the cases he was working on. Josh could sense the level of worry in her voice. He looked at her carefully and could see a tired and stressed lady. He wondered if this was also age showing its effects. How long had it been since he'd really sat and talked to his mother and taken note of how she was growing wearier each year? He had been working long hours and hadn't visited every second weekend like he'd used to. Work had consumed him over the years.

"I'm going to speak to Dad about the investments later," he said. "We will get to the bottom of this, Mom, I promise!" he reassured her.

"Thank you, my boy," she said and held his arm.

The cars went out onto the track for the qualifying session. Josh took out his phone and started the stopwatch, checking every lap time his father did. Alan was doing well.

"He will be at least top three for the start of the first race," Josh guessed.

"Yay, go Uncle Alan!" yelled Daniel.

The actual times were released by the official timesheets and confirmed Alan had placed third for the start of the race. The first five cars were separated by split seconds. It was going to be an exciting race. They walked down the stairs to the pits to meet Josh's father.

Elizabeth fetched a present from her handbag for Daniel. She spoiled him like a grandson. He sat on a blanket on the floor and played with the toy race cars that he'd just opened. Josh and his father went for a walk. They talked about the race ahead and what the strategy was going to be and came up with a game plan to pass the two cars ahead of him.

"Mom told me about your retirement funds invested in Hillstrong Holdings," Josh said.

"I don't know what to say. If I say it once then I've said it a hundred times: I would never have signed that document. It makes no financial sense."

Josh believed him. Could it have been a careless mistake? His mom told him that he was making mistakes lately, mistakes that he never used to make. Forgetfulness, saying things that didn't make sense – clear signs of ageing.

"I agree, Dad. I don't believe it either. I suspect foul play. Make me copies of your file at home with all your investment papers and I'll take a look and see if there is anything that we might have missed. I will also look into the broker and see if there is anything against his name. However, if this nightmare turns out to be real, Dad, there isn't going to be any ground to be made up from

Hillstrong Holdings. It's a terrible situation." Josh rested his hand on his father's shoulder.

"Thanks, boy. That would be great!" He accepted his son's offer out of desperation. He was always a man who would handle his own affairs and wouldn't reach out for help.

Josh was glad to be able to be of some help to his father even in such a sickening situation. He, of course, had relied on his parents for everything growing up: first car, university fees, and first house, all with the help of his parents. His parents weren't wealthy by any means, but had given Josh everything that they hadn't had as children.

"Alright, let's get back to the racing and bring a trophy home tonight," Josh said and walked back to the pits to prepare for the race. Josh walked Daniel around the race car, explaining all the different aspects of racing, from the brakes to the suspension system and then the computer switches inside the cockpit of the race car. Once Daniel was satisfied that the race car was ready for the race, it was time to line up in the pits. Alan went out on the formation lap and stopped on the grid in third position. There was eight laps for him to manoeuvre past the first two places. The cars were very evenly matched and so it would come down to consistent racing and looking for any opportunity.

The race cars on the starting grid roared their engines, the lights lit up row by row until they all went out, signalling the start of the race. Everyone made a successful start with no stationary cars left on the grid. The first three laps were all very similar, with Alan right on the bumper of the cars ahead of him, applying pressure. On the fourth lap he managed to pass the third place, making him second place and then on the fifth lap he made a move that put him in first place, only to run wide and be passed by both drivers again.

It was some of the closest racing that Josh had ever watched with his father behind the wheel. The first two cars were battling each other as well as driving defensively against Josh's father. It was in the second last lap that Josh's father attempted a move at each corner, but was blocked by the leaders. There were three corners left of the race. Alan held his nerve and accelerated late into a corner that would place him on the inside of the drivers ahead but, knowing the track, Josh knew that this move would only place him on the outside of the next corner, giving the other drivers the better racing line and therefore the advantage. Josh wasn't sure what the other option was from his vantage point. It seemed like game over.

Seconds before the corner Josh watched his father change direction and racing lines and switch to the outside of the corner, dummying his previous move the other drivers had already committed to defending. He had the speed from the straight and went around the drivers on the outside. His car was no faster than the others and so he had to rely on his racing line for the lead.

He managed to get next to the leaders and was positioned on the inside of the final corner. He made the move across the apex of the final corner and then it was his turn to drive defensively and hold position. It was a smart move that gave Alan Carter the victory of the day. Josh sat there overjoyed for his father but at the same time he realised that his father still had a very sharp mind. There was no way he could have made the investment mistakes that he was accused of.

Josh and Daniel did not stay for the prize-giving but decided to head back home because Gabby would be missing them. After a long day in the sun and with the noise of all the race cars, Daniel fell asleep not ten minutes into the drive home. They arrived home to a dinner cooked by Gabby, who was eagerly waiting for them. Josh carried Daniel inside and assured Gabby that he had eaten well throughout the day so she didn't have to wake him for dinner.

She put Daniel to bed and returned to the kitchen. Josh gave Gabby a run-down of the race day and showed her the photos that he and Daniel had taken together.

"I'm so glad that Daniel has this boy bonding time with you. As much as I want to spend every day with you guys, I think it's important for him, and you, to have some guy time!" she said. Gabby reached for Josh's hand.

They retreated to the couch to watch some TV, chatting and sitting together with Gabby's legs on Josh's lap. Josh told Gabby about the conversation that Daniel had had with him in the car that morning. Gabby was hardly surprised. She knew that Daniel was a mature boy for his age. She was, however, a bit sad to hear of the memories that Daniel had of her fighting with her ex-husband. He hardly ever brought that up with her.

Josh and Gabby were home-bodies. They enjoyed the simple act of staying home and being in each other's company. She felt herself slipping more and more into the arms of Josh, both figuratively and literally, while they cuddled each other.

"So Daniel thinks we're boyfriend and girlfriend?" she teased.

"Apparently so."

"How does that make you feel?"

"To have you seen by people as my girlfriend?"

"Yes?"

"Are you kidding me? Fantastic! I would be proud to be your boyfriend," he said.

"Well then, it's settled," said Gabby and kissed Josh deeply.

CHAPTER FOURTEEN

Breach of Mandate

JOSH'S FATHER HAD DROPPED OFF his file of investment documents earlier in the morning, Josh had quickly reviewed the contents of the file and made an appointment with the investment broker as soon as possible. The offices of Nicholas Webster were in a modern office park in Illovo, Johannesburg. Josh parked his BMW next to a red Ferrari that he assumed could only be Nicholas'. The front of the glass doors were sandblasted with phrases such as "Investments" and "Your financial future in our hands". He grabbed his meeting binder and entered the building, greeted the receptionist at the front desk, and asked to see Mr Webster, telling her he had made an appointment to see him.

"Sir, please take a seat while I tell Mr Webster that you have arrived," said the young receptionist. She was pretty, and by the manner that she was pressing all the wrong buttons on the phone system to speak to her boss, gave Josh the impression that she couldn't be that bright and was not hired for her competence. Josh looked around the office. To his surprise, it was modest. He supposed that most of the profits were in that red Ferrari outside.

All the furniture appeared to have been ordered from the same corporate furniture retailers. He wouldn't be surprised if they were all Hillstrong Holdings branded. He looked under the chair that he was sitting on and under the seat was the engraving "HH". He was correct. On the walls were various framed, laminated certificates comprising a Financial Service Provider licence and next to it a Certificate for Excellent Service from some financial magazine that Josh had never heard of. By law every institution providing financial advice was obliged to have the license on the wall in the entrance for customers to see, similar to a liquor licence in a bar.

An office door opened and a man with long, greasy dark hair, unshaven and blinged out with a gold chain and a heavy-looking gold wristwatch, walked towards him as he greeted him.

"Josh Carter! The legal legend here in my offices. What a privilege! How are you doing, big guy?"

Josh gave a forced smile. Big guy? He disliked Nicholas Webster already. What was this? High school football talk?

"Mr Webster, nice to meet you!"

"Please come into my office," Webster said, gesturing through the same door he had just walked out of.

His office was fancier than the reception area. He had a large office that was a boardroom, office and lounge area all in one. There were no books behind his desk, nor anything that would lead one to believe he was intelligent. Instead, there were autographed memorabilia of various sports stars, signed rugby balls and jerseys, and even horse racing photos. Below all the memorabilia was a liquor cabinet with glass doors that contained whiskey bottles and tumbler glasses.

Webster waited for the door to close and then started the meeting. "Please have a seat anywhere that you are comfortable."

Josh looked around at the various options. He wanted to make it clear that it wasn't a social visit and so he decided on the boardroom table.

"My receptionist, Mandy, said that when you called to make the appointment you told her that you wanted to discuss the matters of one of my existing clients, Alan Carter, who I can only imagine is your father?"

"That is correct. My father lost a lot of money with the Hillstrong Holdings crash and I would like to take a look at his file with the investment documentation and instructions."

"Unfortunately, Mr Carter, I wish you had brought him along because I cannot share any client files without the client being present or giving me written permission for same."

This line was all too well rehearsed, as Josh expected. He was prepared for these stalling tactics and took out a document from his meeting binder and handed it to the broker.

"Power of Attorney on behalf of my father. I am authorised to request and review all documents to do with his investments."

It was clear that Webster was caught off guard by this and was very uncomfortable. "Mr Carter, I have discussed this matter with your father and I explained to him that it was very unfortunate that he lost most of his retirement funds. It's the risk we take when funds are invested in a high risk, high reward investment like his were. I have all the documents to prove it."

He walked behind his desk where a filing cabinet stood, pulled out the file and handed it to Josh. Josh scanned through the documents and found that, on the papers explaining the high risk, high reward investment schemes, the pages were not initialled but at the bottom of the final page was what appeared to be his father's signature. These pages did not appear in the file that his father had given him. He closed the file on the boardroom table.

"Mr Webster – "

" – Please, call me Nick."

"Alright, Nick. For how long have you managed my father's investments?"

"About one and a half years."

"And before that he was very meticulous about diversifying his investments in which he had a thirty-twenty-fifty split of high, medium and low risk portfolios. He had done very well for himself over the years with that strategy and now his risk is ninety-ten in high risk and medium risk and nothing in low risk at all, which was his most valuable investment pool. It just doesn't make sense why he would take on all that risk right before retirement?"

"Josh, my man, I'm sorry for your father's loss of funds. I have had this same conversation with many investors who lost their life savings because of the Hillstrong Holdings scandal. It happens all the time. I wouldn't call it a mid-life crisis but sometimes my clients are looking for a bit more excitement. They take on the risk and sometimes it pays off and sometimes it doesn't. They dream of the retirement that they want and I make sure I provide them with all the documentation on the risks and consequences. It's all in the file there."

Alan Carter looking for excitement by gambling with his retirement funds? That would be the day, thought Josh.

"Mr Web... Nick, that doesn't sound like my father at all. He wouldn't stake his and my mother's retirement like that."

"Woah, big guy, I don't like what you are implying here. Are you saying that I haven't been above board with your father's investments? I don't appreciate these accusations at all."

Again with the "big guy" comment. If he says that again I might just sock him in the mouth. Josh thought to himself as his temper was rising, but he could not afford to let it get the better of him, not let a personal reaction get in the way.

"I'd like a copy of his file. Once I have reviewed it I will come back and discuss with you."

"Of course. I have nothing to hide. Unfortunately, our printer is offline at the moment. I will make the copies as soon as it's sorted and you can come pick up the file tomorrow."

"Thank you. I appreciate your time, Nick. I will be in touch." Josh didn't extend his hand for a shake but instead got up and left the office. He walked past Mandy, the receptionist, who was collecting printed documents from the printer, and left the building.

On his way home he dialled Detective Sidd.

Sidd picked up on the second ring. "Sidd," he answered in a very detective-like manner.

"Mark, hi, it's Josh. I have a favour to ask." He filled Detective Sidd in on the situation.

"Sounds like a real money-hungry sleaze ball. I'll do a background check on him and let you know what I can find."

"Thanks, Mark. He hasn't been honest with me either. He lied about the printer not working when I asked for a copy of my father's portfolio. I'm worried he will dispose of the documents or forge them further."

"Go speak to any judge who you think will grant a search warrant, and do it fast!" said Sidd.

"Thanks, Mark. I'll get on it immediately." Josh put the phone down and then starting calling every person whom he knew working at the court house and was told that the soonest he could have a search warrant signed off and implemented was in the next few days. It was good enough for Josh, considering it was a personal favour. Josh called Gabby to ask whether she wanted to go for lunch, but she couldn't. She was showing houses all afternoon. He decided he would go to Isabelle's and have lunch with Vee.

He arrived at Isabelle's. The restaurant was quiet, preparing for the night-time rush. Almost every table would require a reservation. Vee looked up from behind the bar and gave him a warm smile. She was speaking to her staff about the evening's events, and she was always so well prepared for every evening. She gestured to him to sit in the corner booth where they always sat and that she would be with him in five minutes. A waiter who noticed this exchanged instantly seated him and passed him a menu.

"Hi Josh, you hungry for lunch or are you just having drinks?" said a pretty woman dressed as a waitress who Josh had been served by many a time.

"Hi, Eloise, I'm famished. Wouldn't mind the house burger special and a coke, please." He handed her back the closed menu.

"Coming right up!" she said and walked to the kitchen to place the order.

Josh called his parents and updated them on the meeting with Nicholas Webster. He wasn't happy with the feelings he had and assured them he was looking deeper into it. His parents thanked him for his help. They sounded scared and desperate and it killed Josh to hear them so down and worried.

"I am so glad to see your friendly face again!" said a familiar voice.

Vee stood by Josh's table with outstretched arms.

Josh stood up and hugged Vee. "Vee, sorry I haven't come by, it's just been such a mad-house," he said as they sat down together.

"Please, don't apologise at all. I just mean it's so good to see you."

"Thanks for all the food that you sent with Gabby when I was discharged from hospital. I was not able to leave the house much for the first few days and it definitely helped to have delicious food!" said Josh.

"Oh, of course, it was the least I could do for you. Did you get your suit jacket? I figured you would want that back sometime," she said with an almost inquisitive demeanour, fishing for a reaction.

"Oh yes, thanks, I had forgotten about it, actually," said Josh. For a moment Josh thought that Vee seemed a bit disappointed that he didn't elaborate on the situation, but maybe Josh was reading too much into it.

Josh and Vee caught up over lunch. They spoke about everything, as usual: restaurant, work and love life.

Josh didn't provide any compromising details about his work but gave her a general update. He gave more details about him and Gabby.

"She sounds like a nice girl, Joshy!" she said affectionately while placing her hand on his arm.

Josh confided in Vee in everything, and he did again during lunch. With Gabby living with him he had fallen more deeply for her and Daniel and the three of them had become a family. It was everything he had been waiting for. He told Vee that Gabby was looking for a bigger house for him, one big enough for the three of them, and that he planned on asking her and Daniel to move in permanently with him.

Vee removed her hand from Josh's arm but encouraged his plans and expressed no doubt that he should go for it. She spoke about the restaurant and how well it was doing. It continued to get good reviews. She did not have any love in her life but seemed content with that. Once the restaurant became busier, Josh left Vee to her job. He pecked her on her cheek and assured her that he wouldn't leave it this long again before visiting again. He left Isabelle's with Vee watching him and gently wiping a tear from her eye. It was happiness for him and also sadness for her because he had found something so great and she wanted him to be happy, but she was not destined to be that person who brought such happiness to him.

CHAPTER FIFTEEN

Gym Thugs

JOSH WAS UP EARLY AND sweating at the gym. The day's session was a high intensity workout that consisted of sprints, box jumps, and some cross-fit exercises for strength. He was getting back into his gym routine slowly and was starting to feel like himself again, although he was distracted by the previous day's meeting with his parents' investment broker. As he was performing his clean and snatch exercises, with the heavy barbell over his head, he plotted out a plan of action against Webster.

He had an ability to retreat into his mental bubble and construct a plan of action while performing other tasks. His mind never switched off. It had been during a personal best five kilometre sprint on the treadmill that he'd come up with his impressive closing argument for one of his previous high profile cases.

He would need just cause for a search warrant of Webster's home and office, especially the home. He should also take a look into that receptionist's background. Something about her bothered him too, and often-times where the solo business owner was up to no good, the assistant was in cahoots with him. It made the whole operation easier to get away with when there was a partner in crime, literally.

Josh moved to the bench press machine next to two heavily steroided men who were twice his size and full of tattoos and who were grunting with each rep of the bar. They had hairy, polony-sized arms and were sweating profusely. The large men were lifting a barbell with two twenties and a ten on each side, totalling 120 kilograms. He could smell them from a few metres away.

Not bad, Josh thought. And, just as he would put his foot flat on the accelerator when driving his car next to a possible petrol head on the road, he added extra plates to his own barbell as well. Competition drove him, made his world go around.

Making sure he was sufficiently warmed up with two sets to stretch his chest, he matched the big men's weight and began his bench press. With no grunts but with controlled breathing, Josh lowered the bar to his chest and pressed upwards while exhaling, for four reps, then five, then six, and finished at ten. He placed the barbell back on the rack noticing a few gym members watching him.

He got up and removed the clips on the end of the barbell which held the weights steady and removed the two ten plates from either side, replacing them with twenties. Now he had 140 kilograms on the barbell. The large men next to him, without saying a word, accepted the challenge and added weights to match his.

He turned his thoughts back to the investigation. He would have to search all of the business deals that Wikus Louw had negotiated in the name of Hillstrong Holdings for at least the last decade. Given the nature of the koi symbol, he would be looking for mergers and acquisitions involving Chinese or Japanese conglomerates in the furniture retail sector.

He knew the growth potential required for a business acquisition made it worth it. Given Hillstrong Holdings market reach, the other company would also need to have a company or group value in the billions for it to be worth Wikus' interest.

The koi ornament was most interesting to him. Symbols like that were often presented in good faith during negotiations of business deals, generally in deals worth hundreds of millions or billions of Rand, the type of deals that Wikus Louw was famous for. The question was, could the findings of Hung Industries be the silver bullet they were looking for, proving foul play by Wikus Louw?

He lay back on the bench and gripped the barbell tightly and, with a deep breath, prepared his mind to push the heavy weight up off the rack, lowering the bar to his chest while inhaling. Now the difficult part. While exhaling and pressing with all his might, he raised the barbell from his chest until his arms were extended, then brought it down again to his chest and up again, repeating this for ten reps again, before placing the bar on the rack.

The two large, sweaty and smelly men next to him took turns to lie on the bench and press the weights. Before one of them lay down, the other would psyche him up by slapping him through the face to make him angry. The one benching would start each set by making a loud grunt for everyone to hear.

The large man lying on the bench took a few exaggerated deep breaths and shouted a self-motivational phrase: "Come on, light weight baby, here we go!" The rest of the gym watched as he lowered the bar and raised it again with a loud grunt, breathing heavily each time. His gym partner stood over him in case of the need of assistance and shouted at him. He managed four reps when his arms started shaking and would not allow a further rep. The bar dropped to the man's chest. With him unable to lift it, his gym partner had to come to his rescue. Red faced and embarrassed, the man walked away, unable to bring himself to even unpack the weights on the bar after his failed set.

Josh watched the two men leaving the gym while he sat back on his own bench, preparing for another set. The men walked past a nearby window in the parking lot and climbed into a car. The one driving had his arm outside the window when Josh noticed that the he had a tattoo on the inside of his forearm. It was a snake slithering through the eye sockets of a human skull. Josh ran to the window to take down the details of the car's plates, but he was just too late.

***

On his way from the gym to his office Josh made a call to Detective Sidd to tell him what he had just discovered and ask for an update on the background search on Nicholas Webster and his receptionist Mandy. He was informed that it was still under way. Detective Sidd added that he was on his way to Josh's office to get through more stacks of documents that were collected by the search and seizure operation.

The men met at Josh's office and made themselves comfortable in the War Room that was taking the form of a fully-fledged criminal and commercial investigation. The room was vastly different to before the operations team had set up the investigation's filing cabinets and items seized in this boardroom. There were six large filing cabinets bolted to the walls of the boardroom and large trunks with padlocks on them that contained anything other than paper documents.

They discussed the business as a whole and all the interested people employed by and associated with Wikus Louw and Hillstrong Holdings. They drew an organogram on two large white-boards and added photos and short descriptions on each role and person. This would assist the men with maintaining an overview of the investigation as a whole, while delving into the detail at the same time.

They divided up the work between them and set to work. Shirley was back at work, and happily so as well. Josh made note of all the evidence collected. With the printing rights granted by the government and prosecutor's office, Shirley, also a great organiser, had printed the various folders on the secure drive created by the operations team and filed them in the steel filing cabinets while Josh was recovering at home from his hospital stay.

An entire cabinet was dedicated solely for the office at the home of Wikus Louw, and was allocated to Josh. He opened the first drawer. Twenty tabs held emails by date, covering a period of five years. He would review each and every one of them. He looked at the whiteboard displaying the people of interest. At the very top of the drawn out pyramid diagram was Wikus Louw. The picture portrayed him at a horse racing event in which one of his racehorses had taken victory. The look of wealth oozed from his smile as he held up a trophy and a large cheque for five million Rand. Confetti flew around in the background.

Beneath him on the whiteboard were the executive team of Hillstrong and members of the board of directors. On the side of that board, Josh drew two stick-men and labelled them "gym thugs" as a reminder to look into who they were.

On the other whiteboard was a timeline and description of mergers and business deals that Hillstrong had been a part of in the last five years. Each group structure would have to be analysed for a possible link.

Detective Sidd, on the other hand, was tasked in performing background checks on all of the persons of interest using the police database. It was unlikely that any of the persons would come up with anything other than parking tickets at most. The level at which these businessmen played the game of life would preclude them from having any kind of criminal record. Knowing what their reputation meant to them would lead to possible bribes and side deals being concluded to ensure their records remained clean.

Shirley made her way in and out of the War Room throughout the day, adding to the filing cabinets and delivering coffee and biscuits from time to time. She was the only other person with access to the documents.

Josh received a text from Gabby asking what time he would be home, to which he replied: "Late. Making progress with Mark. Don't wait up. xx." She sent a further message with just, "Good Luck. xx."

Seeing the response gave Josh a sense of security and groundedness, knowing that he had a supportive partner waiting for him at home.

The men trolled through the stacks of documents with hardly any breaks. Every now and then they would discuss certain pieces of evidence and decide whether it would make its way onto the material documents pile that would possibly require further investigation or whether it would be immediately added to the case that would be presented for the arrest of Wikus Louw and his associates. They worked until late into the evening until they could no longer concentrate on the documents before them. The room looked a mess. Heaps of documents in piles, with coloured sticky notes categorising them into different evidence categories, were scattered across the twenty-seater boardroom table, and empty take-away boxes were piled into the trash bin in the corner.

Josh went to his office and opened his minibar fridge in the corner on the floor and removed two beers. The men went out onto the balcony with the view of the city beneath them. The office had an incredible view of Sandton. It was one of the deciding factors that had made Josh ultimately purchase the space; the view alone was worth the hefty mortgage. It had taken him five years to pay it off by being extremely frugal with his money and making his debt a priority each month. The first month following the date he paid it off he went straight to the BMW dealership and ordered the BMW M4 that was parked outside Carter & Associates at that very moment.

The men sat on deck chairs and looked out at the city lights of the various skyscrapers and lonely cars. Josh usually sat alone on the balcony. They could see the few people high in their glass towers also burning the midnight oil and the night shift cleaning personnel getting the offices ready for a new business day when the sun came up. They spoke about their personal lives involving their families.

Detective Sidd was married with a daughter of eight years old. His daughter was tomboyish and wanted to be a policeman, just like her dad, and was the apple of his eye. His wife, Karen, was a kindergarten teacher who was also his high school sweetheart. They'd met in the tenth grade and had never looked at another person since.

They had been through a rough life with him being on the force. She feared for his life every day on the job, especially in the early years when he was obliged to do street patrol and raids on criminal territories, mostly involving drug dealers in the flats in dodgy areas of the city down south. She was so happy for him when he had been promoted to Chief Investigating Officer five years before. It also gave him more normal working hours so that he would be home for dinner on most nights and would be able to attend his daughter's school events on the weekends, and let him have some quality time with his daughter after missing out most of her initial years of upbringing. Things had improved drastically since.

"Do you miss the action of the early days?" Josh asked him.

"Yes and no. I still see the bigger picture in what I'm doing. I may not put myself in danger as much as before, and feel the adrenalin of the higher purpose in the moment, but after an investigation has been concluded and a criminal has been brought to justice I realise that it all is worth it in the end," he answered.

Josh retrieved more beers from his mini fridge in his office and set them down on the table between them. "What was the deciding factor for you to have more of a desk job?"

"I lost my partner while I was still a rookie. We were a month away from graduation onto the force. He was my best friend and we were patrolling together. He was more reckless, something he saw as brave. 'Gung-ho', we called him. He thought he was bullet proof. He would rave about the close-call busts that he made and that nothing fatal happened to him. He would burst through the door on a raid, sometimes not waiting for backup when it was needed. The other men on the force took bets on how long it would be until he would have an incident that would calm him down. They all refused to partner with him.

"On that particular night we had tailed a suspicious vehicle that had a busted tail-light and what looked like a bullet hole in the boot. Once the driver realised we were on to him, he tried to lose us in the suburbs of Hillbrow, the parts where you don't want to be caught alone in, especially as a cop. We called for backup, but it took too long to get there. The van had been hijacked a few days earlier and had been used in an armed robbery of a cash-in-transit van. Turns out they had called ahead to their crew and, when we cornered them in an abandoned building, we realised that it was actually an ambush.

"It turned into a gun fight. Our car was shot up pretty bad, but we managed to get away on foot. They chased us until we could not run any further. Backup was minutes away when four members of their gang caught us in an alleyway. We had run out of bullets and they had not. They made us kneel execution style. I thought it was my last night on this earth.

"My partner wasn't the type of man to go out on his knees. He struggled with them, so I got up too and we fought them hard until

I heard a shot and I saw my partner freeze. It was as if the world stood still. We both knew what had happened.

"He fell to the ground as backup arrived. The officers took the four men out, but it was too late for my partner. If we'd just managed to stall for another half a minute things would have probably turned out different. I sat there in the alleyway with my partner bleeding out in my arms. He was so afraid. The fearless man looked at me and trembled, begged me to save his life, but the bullet had struck a main artery and the blood couldn't be stopped. I still remember the warm sensation as the blood poured over me. Worst night of my life.

"I was given a few months' leave, which I took. I was eager to get back out there, not to avenge my partner but to continue to make a difference. Once I was cleared, I put in an application for the commercial crimes unit and took the tests. I found my place in a team of dedicated individuals which has led me here. I've never looked back since."

They opened one last beer each and brainstormed the investigation at hand.

CHAPTER SIXTEEN

Search and Seizure

Josh's phone woke him as it vibrated on his bedside table. It was an incoming call from Detective Sidd. The warrant for the search and seizure on the home and office of Nicholas Webster was approved and a team was being assembled immediately. If Josh wanted to tag along, he should be ready in half an hour and Detective Sidd would pick him up on the way. Josh responded in the affirmative. He opened the door to Gabby and Daniel's room slightly to see them fast asleep. He left a note for Gabby on the kitchen counter, left the house, and minutes later was picked up in the police cruiser.

"Morning," Detective Sidd said and handed Josh a takeaway coffee he had picked up on his way.

"Has anyone told you what a legend you are?" Josh said.

Detective Sidd nodded and filled Josh in on the latest information that had been uncovered. Nicholas was divorced and father of a three-year-old girl. "We contacted his wife, or should I say ex-wife, and was informed that he had abandoned them, no maintenance payments, nothing. They don't know where he went. He just picked up and left one day. They live in Cape Town where our boy used to live. And get this, Webster is not his real name. His surname is Nel."

Josh drank his coffee and took in all the information without interrupting the story.

"It gets better. He is sleeping with his receptionist, Mandy. Our private investigator guy took some snaps of the two of them two days ago when she went home with him. She lives with her parents, but stays over at his place most nights. Yesterday, our guy lost track of them; said the two of them left work around lunch time and never returned."

They joined the team that was set up outside the investment broker's office. Another team would search his home simultaneously. They didn't expect to find anyone at the office in the early hours of the morning. They entered the office and searched the building. They confiscated all of the files in the filing cabinets that were mostly empty – either Nicholas Webster did not have many clients at all or he had destroyed most of his clients' files.

Josh was relieved to find that his father's file was still in the cabinet and that led him to believe the former scenario was most likely. Once the documents were itemised, Josh used the broker's own office printer (which was in perfect working order) to make a copy of the file and gave the search and seizure team back the original.

Detective Sidd received a call from his team at Nicholas Webster's home.

"Wait, Sergeant, let me put you on speaker," Detective Sidd said. "Start again, Sergeant."

"Sir, like I said, the apartment that Mr Nel was renting has been vacated. There are few personal items left, but it is clear that he's left – and in a hurry. We found some woman's clothes on the floor as well. It seems they didn't even wait to pack all of their belongings and dropped some stuff on their way out as well. Half eaten food on the table, television still on, door wasn't locked even. You know the way it goes. We have put out a national search for the two individuals. Hopefully we will pick them up somewhere and be able to bring them in for questioning."

"Thank you, Sergeant. Fill in your report and I will read it later when I am in the office," Sidd instructed.

Josh was angry. "That bastard!" He took the copy of his father's file and went back home.

Gabby was awake and making breakfast, Josh told her about the events of the morning.

"Damnit, that's bad luck. I wonder where they went?" she said and saw the file that Josh had copied earlier lying on the kitchen counter.

"What file is that?" she asked.

"It's a copy of my father's file from the broker's office. I have a file from my father and will compare it to this one, and any additional documents that the broker's file contains may be the phony ones that my dad believes contain a forged signature. After breakfast I'll do the comparison and see what I come up with. What does your day look like?"

"I am seeing a client this morning to show them what I have planned for their interior decorating and then I have the whole afternoon clear. Would you like to have lunch together today? I know you're busy, especially with your parents' broker as well, so if you can't make it it's really okay," she said with not much hope.

Josh hadn't seen much of Gabby lately, even though they were living together in the same house. "Yes, that would be great," he said almost immediately.

She smiled and kissed him on the cheek. "Gotta run," she said as she walked out the door.

Daniel was going to school and so Josh had the house to himself. It was strangely quiet all of a sudden. A bachelor not used to being alone any more. Was he really a bachelor, though? Seemed not.

He made himself coffee and toast with eggs and started reviewing the file. Just as he'd thought, he couldn't find any document in his father's own file with his father's signature that allowed Nicholas Webster to invest the funds in Hillstrong Holdings in the percentages that he had. It should not have been more than thirty percent at the most because the portfolio was supposed to be split into thirty percent high risk and returns only and the remainder was twenty percent medium risk and fifty percent low risk – not a reflection of someone who wanted to gamble their life savings away. He phoned his father and updated him on the developments.

"Hear that, Elizabeth? I told you I wasn't losing my mind. I didn't sign any document. That criminal has committed fraud and lost our money," his father shouted to his mother, who was in another room. Josh reassured his father that he would do everything he could to find the broker and see what money could be recouped, but it was difficult and foolish to promise any success. It would be likely that Nicholas Webster had lost most, if not all, of the money and that was why he was on the run.

Josh returned to the War Room at Carter & Associates and continued with the due diligence investigation into Wikus Louw. He had Shirley compile files of all the latest mergers and acquisitions that involved Wikus Louw and Hillstrong Holdings for the past decade. This included all company filings and news articles of all the transactions. There were many files – that just showed the voraciousness of the transactions concluded by Wikus Louw.

A normal company on the Johannesburg Stock Exchange would conclude one main merger a year or every few years at the most. Wikus Louw's record for the most mergers in one year amounted to fifteen. It was ludicrous. And given what Josh had uncovered about Hung Industries, he knew that most of these merger deals were done without proper legal documentation.

His major interest with the persons of interest at the moment lay with Hung industries. He had just received an email from Rhonda Martins that the next day's briefing session at the Ranch House would include a video conference with Simon Chen and Fei Hung in China. He was hoping that would lead to a major breakthrough with the case. However, even though Hung Industries could shed light on the international transaction that had failed, he would still need to thoroughly investigate the South African arm of the group of companies and tie Wikus Louw and his closest associates to all the unlawful actions of directors of public companies.

CHAPTER SEVENTEEN

Ranch House

JOSH DROVE HIS BMW OVER the now familiar dirt road leading to the Ranch House while Gabby napped in the passenger seat and Daniel was wide eyed at all the nature around him. They had arranged for family accommodation for the three of them and had also requested a night-time game drive. Daniel found the whole experience of entering the reserve fascinating and did not take his eyes from the guards at the gates as they inspected the car and all their luggage, holding their assault rifles at the ready.

Josh explained to Daniel that this was no ordinary reserve experience, but a top secret one. Satisfied that they were a legitimate family going to the Ranch House and not imposters, the guards let them through the gate. After travelling the few kilometres on the dirt road they arrived at the Ranch House. The staff were ready for guests this time and met the three of them outside the building in the open drive-through area. The staff were trained valets and bell-boys and carried all of their luggage. Josh was reluctant to hand over the BMW keys to a young man to park the car but gave in, after a subtle stare down with the young man.

The Carter family were led to their accommodation, a large open plan area with a king size extra-length, four-poster bed with mosquito netting hanging from the rafters, and in a smaller adjoining room a single bed for Daniel, with the same netting placed over it. On the other side of the main room was a large lounge area with couches, coffee tables and book cases, designed to make people feel at home – in a very luxurious home. The room had a balcony that faced the Mkuze River and they could hear the sound of water flowing and cascading over the rocks a few hundred metres below. They walked outside and looked at the South African landscape.

"What an incredible view," said Gabby in appreciation.

"It's the best," Josh commented back. "What do you think, bud? Do you like it?" he asked Daniel.

"It's really wild. Look at all this land. You can see for miles!" he answered excitedly. "I'm going to get my binoculars that mom bought me to see if I can spot any dangerous animals down there!" and off he ran to fetch them. He was at that age where every new experience brought out the possibility to have a future profession in that area of expertise.

Since arriving at the Ranch House, Daniel had changed his dream job three times, from seeing the guards at the gate and wanting to be an army spy, then changing his mind back to being a lawyer like Josh, to what was now being heard from the excited young boy standing on the balcony that, one day when he was big, he would be a game ranger and work at a place like the Ranch House.

Josh and Gabby unpacked their bags while watching Daniel shouting animal spottings to them. Being on the edge of the river was a perfect opportunity to see animals coming to the water to drink. It was also why the beds had to be covered with mosquito nets to protect guests from the threat of malaria. Although Gabby had been excited to be included in the meeting that day, Simon

Chen had requested that only essential members of the team be included in the video conference call. She was going to spend time with Daniel, as she was not comfortable with anyone else looking after her child and also it was a big experience for him being his first time to a private game reserve and she wanted to be with him for that.

The staff walked them around the rest of the Ranch House, showing them the various common areas. There was a lounge/entertainment area, where guests could spend their down time between game drives, a bar that they called the "Watering Hole" for the guests who wanted to socialise, and even a pool outside by the deck area where all meals were enjoyed. That area boasted a view, similar to the one from Josh's room, of the mountains and the Mkuze River.

What an incredible place, Josh thought. He would perform investigations full time for the State if it meant that he could have a getaway like this every once in a while and be there for business. Once satisfied that Gabby and Daniel were well taken care of and were fine to roam around on their own, he made his way to the meeting room where Rhonda Martins and Detective Sidd were waiting for him.

"Hey guys," he greeted.

"Hi Josh," Rhonda Martins answered back. "I am glad to see that you brought your family along, Mark's wife and daughter are also here for the night. I think you guys are going to have a great time together. I hear that there is a game drive planned for later this afternoon. The game ranger was telling me when I arrived that they had spotted a kill a short while ago and that it will be a great day for animal spotting."

"Great, looking forward to it," Josh said while shaking Detective Sidd's hand. "How you doing, Mark?"

"Well thanks, Josh. Yourself? I'll introduce you and Gabby to my wife and daughter after the meeting. Like you, I assume, this is going to be our first family vacation or any vacation for quite some time. They are very excited to be here. Daddy has such an exciting job all of a sudden! It's going to take a lot more effort from my wife to talk my eight-year-old daughter out of joining the police force now," he said, chuckling.

"We've got about fifteen minutes," Rhonda Martins interrupted, "before we connect to Hong Kong to speak with Simon Chen and Fei Hung, so we can have a catch up before we do so. To give you some information on his background, Hung is a business tycoon. He owns many hotels and much real estate now, but it wasn't always his business.

"He, like our friend Wikus Louw, was in the furniture manufacture and retail sector. Our research brought up a time where he was trying to expand this business, which is where he was introduced to Wikus Louw. The two of them were going to merge and form one of the largest networks for manufacturing and retailing of affordable residential furniture for the lower and middle classes across the globe.

"The news articles we managed to dig up and preparatory work that was concluded for the transaction comprised competition filings and legal opinions for a large merger. The financial thresholds, as you know, are that the acquiring firm, Hillstrong Holdings, and the target firm, Hung Industries' combined assets or annual turnover is over R6.6 billion and that Hung industries' assets or annual turnover on its own exceeded R190 million. This threshold was easily met by the parties, from the legal opinion that we read.

"In the months subsequent to these negotiations it appears that he exited the furniture market by selling all of his stock and converting all the premises used for storage of his own products for leasing to other businesses, and also constructed various residential and commercial buildings. Subsequent to that, he went into the hotel business as well.

"Although this decision has been very profitable for Mr Hung, and he has made a large fortune doing so, what I don't understand is that one moment he was concluding a large merger with Hillstrong Holdings, and then he took the drastic step of selling all of his companies' stock and changed business avenues within a few months, which is no easy feat.

"Even though he is extremely well connected in the furniture network, he does not actively trade in it anymore. What we need to determine is, firstly, whether this was a result of his interactions with Wikus Louw, and, secondly, what information did he come across that was such a serious deterrent to staying in that market. We must try lead the conversation with Mr Hung in that direction. And any information that we can obtain on Wikus Louw, as well as any of his associates, is obviously the primary goal.

"Wikus Louw is clearly the primary target of the investigation, but I just don't believe that he acted completely on his own; it's just too much work to be done by one person. So, any information that we obtain from Mr Hung could assist the investigation."

Rhonda flipped a switch and a white awning lowered from the ceiling on the far side of the room, with a projector powering up for the video conference. A blue screen showed that they were waiting for connection. After a minute, the screen's picture changed to present a video feed of a young looking Asian man, dressed smartly, sitting in a large conference room all on his own. He was in his late thirties, with longish hair slicked back and a face with sharp-looking features. In the background, a large window on one side had a view of Hong Kong city, the tops of other skyscrapers barely visible. He was obviously on a very top floor on one of the tallest buildings in the city.

"Good morning, Miss Martins, Detective Sidd, and Mr Carter. My name is Simon Chen, Mr Hung's personal advisor and assistant," he said. The three South Africans greeted back.

"Mr Hung will be with you shortly. He extends his apologies as he had a last minute phone call of an urgent nature. He shouldn't be long now. I confirm that I have briefed Mr Hung on the nature of this discussion today – and that is to provide you with any information on Mr Wikus Louw in the ongoing investigations into his business affairs under the name of Hillstrong Holdings and any related companies. Is this correct?"

It was Rhonda who answered his question. "Yes, Mr Chen, that is correct. We would appreciate any information that could lead to prosecuting Mr Louw for any fraudulent and unlawful actions, as well as any associates who were involved in these activities."

Simon Chen looked to his right suddenly. "Very well, Miss Martins. Mr Hung has arrived." He immediately stood up and pulled out a chair for another man, quite some years older than he was but no less smartly dressed and put together. He was rounder looking, with short black hair.

Simon Chen paused and spoke softly to Fei Hung, who nodded his head in appreciation and sat down to face the screen. Simon Chen stood behind his employer and spoke loudly, "Mr Hung, I introduce to you, from your right to your left, Miss Rhonda Martins, Detective Mark Sidd, and lastly Mr Josh Carter." They all greeted in unison.

"Good morning, gentlemen and lady, my greatest apologies for keeping you waiting. I had to attend to an urgent business matter."

Rhonda Martins started off. "Not at all, Mr Hung. We know that you are an extremely busy man and we are grateful for your time. Shall I start us off?"

"Yes, please do, Miss Martins," he said in a voice deeper than one would expect from a man of such small stature. He placed his hands together and rested them on the table in front of him. His shoulders were upright; the posture must have been drilled into him as a child. His culture was very strict about looking professional at all times.

Josh noticed that Simon Chen had not taken a seat at the boardroom table where many chairs were available but instead took a step backwards and stood against the back of the room with his arms in front of him, hands together and looking straight ahead.

"Mr Hung, as you know from our explanation to Mr Chen as well as from the news globally, Wikus Louw is under investigation for causing the corporate crash of Hillstrong Holdings. The allegations against him are quite serious and the extent of the damage is not yet known. Although we are gathering much evidence in our investigation, we are looking for any additional sources on his business dealings over the many years to determine any unlawful behaviour and a timeline on when he may have started to undermine the law. We are hoping that a forensic financial and legal audit will confirm anything else we find in this regard. You know the global reach of the Hillstrong group of companies and that our investigation will extend across international lines."

"And the reason that you have contacted me is because eight years ago, Hung Industries was in a position to conclude a transaction with Hillstrong Holdings, only to cease the negotiations, much to everyone's surprise?" Fei Hung asked.

"Yes, Mr Hung, that is correct." Rhonda Martins added, "To be completely transparent with you, we found the email correspondence between Mr Simon Chen on your behalf and Wikus Louw that we sent to your offices for your reference. We would like to know what changed your mind so suddenly, and why you did not proceed with the transaction."

"Thank you, Miss Martins, I did receive the email correspondence. I can answer many of your questions. I want, however, to make it clear that I do not wish to become embroiled in these proceedings when they eventually go to a court of law. I will answer your questions and no more. I do not want to be seen as working for the South African government. Equally I do not want to be the man that investigates and provides information on the businessmen and women who I tend to negotiate with. No matter how unethical I may think that person, it is not my place to bring justice to the business world. With respect, that is your job," he stated stiffly. He was clearly distancing himself from Wikus Louw. He did not sound rude, but blunt, to the point.

"Mr Hung, thank you," Josh said. "We understand your position and we do not expect you to become involved any more than providing us with an understanding of your dealings with Wikus Louw and any of his associates."

"Understood, Mr Carter. Shall we begin?" Fei Hung was not a man who wasted time on small talk. His responses were short and he did not say any more than he needed to get his point across.

"Yes, thank you. Firstly, please tell us about your interaction with Wikus Louw over the years and what his business character was."

"I had various interactions with Mr Louw over the years, the first of which was three years before the failed negotiation in respect of the possible merger between Hung Industries and Hillstrong Holdings. Over time, my board paid close attention to Mr Louw as we were alive to the possibility of a merger of our entities. I noticed that Mr Louw, how can I say, was hungry, not only for money, but for power, status and success. This is not in itself a bad quality to have, but all in moderation and as long as it is kept within the bounds of ethical behaviour and lawful transactions.

"The closer we approached the final negotiations of the merger, the clearer it became that the accumulation of the ever-increasing wealth that Mr Louw earned was a source of an egotistical ability to feed the hungry beast of power and his lavish lifestyle. Although he was always very respectful towards my office, our research and observations were that he was a very arrogant man who thought himself invincible. The business risks became riskier and the ethical business lines became more obscured in his dealings."

"Mr Hung, could you elaborate on any of these dealings that would show unlawful transactions?" Josh asked.

"Mr Carter, to be frank with you, the documents and information on Mr Wikus Louw that I may or may not have would not be available to you to be used in any court proceedings. I am very familiar with the rules of South African Courts and I am aware that there are strict rules on the admissibility of evidence. I'm sure you will understand this."

Yes, Josh understood clearly. Fei Hung had used questionable methods to obtain information on Mr Louw as a commercial and personal background check. These methods would in all likelihood include private investigators and information leaked from many business associates of Wikus Louw. Often this would come in dossiers with photographs and wire taps, copied documents, and agreements to which Hung Industries would not be a counterparty and should not be in possession of.

"I understand, Mr Hung. Thank you for your honesty. We would be grateful if you would continue to tell us about your dealings with Wikus Louw personally then."

"Yes. Mr Louw was initially admired by many of my business associates for his fierce negotiation skills and his ability to conclude many transactions annually, year on year, with returns to his investors and shareholders at a very impressive margin.

"We performed a due diligence on Hillstrong Holdings, as can be read in the email correspondence that you have provided my office. In that due diligence we uncovered that Hillstrong Holdings had created an unprecedented level of operational and managerial complexity. Unnecessarily so, in my belief, but then again you people in the West and South Africa do things differently than my people do. However, business can be done not only in one way. What is the saying, Mr Carter? There are many ways to skin a cat. But on that note, in business I would never want to skin a cat at all.

"My thoughts, which were perhaps seen as suspicious at the time, were that a business person as experienced as Mr Louw would know that the simpler a business transaction, the smoother it will flow, like a river without any obstacles. The only reason for any complexity, beyond that of the normal business kind, would be to fool the people on the outside of Hillstrong and quite possibly the people within as well. To distort the facts and procedures followed to conclude transactions.

"I was not taken seriously by my board because of my reputation for being a slightly risk-averse and conservative deal maker – a reputation that I have come to be proud of. It has served my company well over the many years that I have been in charge. However, at the time we were negotiating with Hillstrong Holdings they were ready for a slightly more aggressive strategy for a change. I fear that my board may too have been influenced by the riches and far reach of Mr Louw."

Josh noticed that Simon Chen's posture changed slightly. His facial expression, although just for a second, showed that something Fei Hung had said was not true. Josh continued to listen to Fei Hung and look out for any more signs from his assistant behind him.

"Have you noticed, Mr Carter that any competitor of Hillstrong Holdings in the last decade has either been absorbed by the entity or no longer exists? More peculiar is that once a struggling entity was bought out by Hillstrong, its stock price would increase to the extent that it had purchased a thriving and profit producing company. Despite Hillstrong absorbing a company riddled with debt, its balance sheet would improve. This cannot be, and is not, only due to impressive management and resources. The effects of a poor balance sheet must be reflected in the financial results to the investors and shareholders. This was not the case.

"It was clear that Mr Louw behaved as if the assets of Hillstrong Holdings were the assets of his own. Once a merger had taken place, he would treat Hung Industries as if it were his own too. I could not let that happen. I have a duty to my shareholders that I would protect their investment. I believe that I have done so." Fei Hung stared straight into the video conference camera without expression. He had a poker face and he gave away nothing more than the words that were spoken by him.

"Mr Hung, when carrying out a search and seizure operation at the home of Wikus Louw, amongst many documents and correspondence we found one interesting object – a gold ornament in the shape of a fish, a koi to be exact, with the phrase, 'Become the Dragon'. We would like to know..."

Josh could not finish his question because Simon Chen stepped forward immediately and interrupted the discussion to whisper something into Mr Hung's ear. Mr Hung stood up. "My apologies, Mr Carter, Miss Martins and Detective Sidd, it appears that something urgent requires my attention. Unfortunately, I do not feel that I can be of much more help. I wish you success in your investigation further." Fei Hung and Simon Chen left the room before the three South Africans were able to say goodbye. They switched off the video feed.

"That was sudden," Josh said. "He spoke a lot but didn't really say anything of substance."

Rhonda and Detective Sidd were of the same mind.

"Very peculiar. There were many more questions I was hoping to have him answer for us," said Detective Sidd.

Josh wondered whether the line of questioning about the gold koi ornament was something they did not wish to continue with or whether there truly was an urgent situation.

"So, what was helpful," said Rhonda, "was that Fei Hung and Simon Chen appear to be in possession of very damaging information, although not obtained through legal channels. We need to get our hands on that information somehow."

"Agreed," said Josh. "My first thought would have been to offer him money, but that wouldn't work in this scenario. What can you offer a billionaire when he already has everything he needs?"

"There is always a price, Josh. It may not be money, but there will always be something. We just need to find out what it is," said Detective Sidd. "It could even be dirt that we could use as leverage."

Rhonda finished off the meeting, "That's our homework for today. Other than that we continue pursuing all leads and reviewing all evidence in our possession, maybe we can find some puzzle pieces for the story in the process. For now, you two go meet your families and have a break."

CHAPTER EIGHTEEN

Private Game Reserve

Josh and Detective Sidd left the conference room to find Gabby, Daniel, and Detective Sidd's wife and daughter by the pool.

Gabby raised her head from watching Daniel swimming and saw Josh walking over.

"Hey you," she said.

"Hey you back," said Josh.

"Josh, let me introduce you to my wife, Karen, and that's my daughter, Maddy."

"Nice to meet you, Josh," Karen said. "So you are the person keeping my husband away from home late at night. I'm glad you don't have longer blonde hair," she joked.

Josh chuckled and Detective Sidd just waved it off. "Nice to meet you, Karen. Mark has told me all about you."

Detective Sidd sat down next to his wife and kissed her gently. She placed her arm around him and rested her head on his shoulder. Josh watched them with each other. That was real love, the type that lasts for a lifetime. He went to join Gabby on her deck chair. She was in such a happy place, soaking up the sun and more relaxed than he had ever seen her. "Are you having a good time?" he asked.

"The best," she said simply and smiled at him and reached for his hand. "Maddy and Daniel made friends the moment they met and they haven't stopped talking and playing since. Karen is a wonderful lady, too. I really like her. We spoke to the reserve's staff and arranged a dinner table out here under the stars for the six of us tonight."

"Sounds great," said Josh, laying back next to her with his arm around her while watching the kids play in the pool. Two sweet-hearted kids, splashing in the water and getting to know each other. Daniel seemed more grown up with Maddy around, even though she was a year older, he tried to compensate for that with his boyish behaviour, protecting her from the dangers of the pool cleaning machine and whatever may be floating nearby. Maddy played the damsel in distress and enjoyed the attention.

Josh leaned against Gabby and smelt her hair. Her perfume was the same one she'd worn on the night of the networking event, which brought back memories of her in her black lingerie. He longed for her, to kiss her deeply, touch her skin and undress her.

She removed her sunglasses and looked into his eyes. She seemed to be thinking along the same lines. "I missed you," she whispered softly to him.

"You did, did you? I might have missed you a bit too."

She didn't hit him playfully like she usually would. Instead she leaned in and kissed him on the mouth. Her lips were so soft. Josh could taste some cocktail drink that she had earlier by the fruity flavour on her lips. He'd forgotten that they weren't alone until one of the staff of the reserve interrupted them. "Excuse me, sirs and madams, the game ranger has informed us that he will have the game vehicle ready for the afternoon drive at 3:30PM, after which he will bring you back to the lodge for dinner, which we will prepare for you under the stars, as requested by the beautiful ladies," he said with an air of professionalism.

"Thank you," everyone responded.

"The waiters will be with you shortly to offer you more drinks and snacks. Lunch will be served in two hours, after which you will have roughly an hour to relax before the game drive," he added before walking away.

The waiters arrived and took everyone's drinks orders and informed them that they would be having a cheese and bread platter, and a range of fresh fruit set out by the pool for everyone. The children played in the pool, the two couples drank and joked and unwound together.

The women teamed up against the guys and the guys did not put up much of a fight but instead enjoyed the jovial atmosphere and how happy they were to be relaxing for a change with two beautiful women as company.

The pool deck had a balcony with a view of a beautifully green South African landscape. In the distance you could see mountains and green grass and trees that stretched as far as the eye could see. Down below the balcony was a flowing river where a few buck were drinking, and two hippos were floating in the water in the shade of the trees on the riverbank. The birds were chirping all around them. Daniel and Maddy were now playing game ranger and spotting animals down below, getting more and more excited for the game drive.

They all had lunch and waited for the game ranger to fetch them.

As the heat of the day subsided, the vehicle left the lodge with the six passengers. They drove out into the wild. The game vehicle had three rows of seats. Right in front on the lowest row were Daniel and Maddy, behind them and slightly raised were Detective Sidd and Karen, and right at the back on the top level were Josh and Gabby. Every now and then the game ranger would stop the vehicle to describe how an animal was behaving and what the significance of its markings were.

They saw giraffe eating leaves from the tops of the trees and many small groups of warthog families running through the bushes with their tiny legs sprinting and tails in the air.

"Pumba!" shouted Daniel and Maddy in unison and laughed.

Gabby and Josh sat together enjoying the breeze of the drive, each with a hand on the other's lap. As the sun went down they were treated to a beautiful red and orange sunset that South Africa is so famous for, especially out in the wild. The heat finally subsided the moment the sun went down. The night time air was cool upon their faces as the game vehicle proceeded on. The passengers were given blankets to cuddle under and keep warm.

They were fortunate enough to see two of the big five. A herd of elephant made their way across the reserve and caused destruction to everything in their path. The larger ones pushed over tree trunks and broke branches. Just before the end of the drive they found themselves in a group of over one hundred buffalo, grazing on the far side of the mountain. It was incredible to be so close to such large animals. The game ranger switched off the vehicle and asked everyone to remain silent for a few moments.

"It is quiet, don't you think?" he asked. They all nodded. He continued with his explanation. "But if you listen carefully, it is actually not quiet at all." It took a while for everyone's hearing to adjust, but once it did the various sounds were clear to everyone. They could hear the Buffalo snorting and many insects in the long grass. In the distance far away were the sounds of trees cracking and being pushed over by the herd of elephant and, if you tuned in to it, the constant running of the water down the waterfall and onto the rocks could be heard.

They made their way back to the lodge for dinner. As they exited the vehicle, the waiting staff handed them hot hand towels to wash their dusty hands in preparation for dinner. The table was set up outside with candles and the set menu. The children lay their blankets out on the grass and made a picnic next to the table that was set out romantically for the adults. The adults ordered wine while waiting for their food.

"Cheers everyone. To new friends and a great day," said Josh. They all clinked glasses and drank to each other.

"So, Josh, why did you choose law?" Karen asked.

"It's all I've ever wanted to do. As far as I can remember I have always wanted to be a lawyer. I suppose it was the romance of it initially. You know, the suits, the high profile of being a person in need, and money. Until I started studying. Then I realised I could make a difference, and at the same time make some money," he laughed. "When I started working it was clear to me that if I worked hard it would be something I could be good at. It gave me a kind of purposeful feeling, as if I had found my calling. I love working for myself and having no one to answer to, except for clients. I couldn't be happier."

They all discussed their careers and how they'd ended up where they were and where they would like to see themselves in a few years.

The evening drew to a close. The night was quiet, except for the insects in the immediate vicinity and the flowing water down below. The children had fallen asleep on the blankets while trying to count the stars. When they had emptied their glasses Gabby said, "Thanks for a great day and evening, guys. I think we should get Daniel to bed now; it's getting cold outside."

"We'd better get going too," said Karen. "We had such a great time with you two. I hope to do it again sometime, maybe back in Johannesburg."

"Definitely, we would love that too," said Josh. He stood up and walked to the children sleeping on the blanket. He picked up Daniel, said goodnight to Karen and Detective Sidd, and carried Daniel to the lodge, with Gabby close behind. He carried Daniel into his room and lay him down on the bed and covered him with a thick duvet and the mosquito netting.

The boy was fast asleep. He had had a long and eventful day. Josh was surprised that Daniel had lasted as long as he had. Perhaps he hadn't wanted to miss out on anything with his new friend, Maddy.

Daniel turned around to find Gabby standing in the doorway watching him. "Hey you," he said.

"That's a real good look on you," she whispered as Josh walked out of the room and closed the door to Daniel's room.

"What look is that?" he asked.

"Being a father," she said and took his hand and walked him to the open doorway to the balcony. The cool breeze blew into the main room and fluttered the mosquito netting about. Gabby looked out from the balcony; the moonlight illuminated the water beneath them. Josh stood behind her, wrapped his arms around her and put his chin on her shoulder. He could smell her sweet scent; the smell of perfume mixed with her natural body odour was intoxicating.

"You know, it takes about thirty minutes for your eyes to adjust properly to see the stars," he said.

She held his arms around hers. "After everything we have been through over the past few weeks, this getaway was exactly what we needed, all three of us. It was so amazing to see Daniel being a kid and playing with someone like a normal child. Being an only child and spending so much time with us, I worry that he is growing up too quickly."

"He's a good kid. You're doing an amazing job, Gabs."

"You've helped more than you know, Josh. I can't tell you how grateful I am to have you in our lives." She was silent suddenly.

"What's on your mind?" he asked.

"It was really scary what happened to you at the networking event. I was so terrified. It felt like a part of me was ripped out when I saw you lying on the floor the way you were. I think Daniel and I have just assumed that you would always be there for us, and the thought of something happening to you, if you were taken from us, is unbearable."

Josh felt her cheek get wet on his. "Hey, Gabs, it all worked out, thanks to you. Everything is fine."

"I know, I just can't stop picturing you in that state. Sometimes I battle to catch my breath. But you're right. Everything is fine, more than fine. It's amazing, really amazing."

Josh took the sleeve of his jacket and wiped her face. "I had such a great time with you and Daniel today," he said.

"So did I," she said, "like a real family," and then she went quiet again.

With his arms around her and his face next to hers, Josh could swear he felt her holding her breath for his reply. "Yes, like a real family, Gabs," he said, feeling her exhale slowly, relaxing. He felt the corners of her mouth rise into a smile against his cheek. He kissed her neck and breathed her in. She was like a drug and he needed his fix.

"Speaking about that horrible night, I remember someone looking unbelievable sexy in her black lingerie. When do you think I'll be able to see that again?" he asked.

She turned around, still in his arms, and put her arms around his neck and gazed into his light blue eyes. "Oh, you liked that little set, did you?" she teased.

"You have no idea. I haven't stopped thinking about you in nothing but that for weeks now," he admitted.

She kissed him softly, pulled his ear to her mouth and whispered to him, "I'm wearing it right now."

He kissed her hard and picked her up. She wrapped her legs around his waist as he carried her from the balcony and into the bedroom.

***

They woke early on Sunday morning with the sun-rays streaming into the bedroom. The balcony doors were still open and the curtains were blowing gently with the breeze. Gabby got up and checked on Daniel, who was still slowly stirring awake. Josh made coffee for them and took it out to the balcony. They sat and watched as the animals made their way to the riverbank to have a morning drink. They looked at one another.

"Don't judge me, my hair must be crazy looking," she said.

"You look like a hot mess," said Josh playfully and she stood up and smacked his arm, but he was too quick for her and pulled her onto his lap. "But you're my hot mess and I still think you're beautiful."

"Very smooth, Mr Carter, very smooth," she said and kissed him as Daniel walked through the balcony doors.

"Morning, bud, you look like you slept well," Josh said.

"I'm starving," was all Daniel said back to them.

They got dressed and made their way to breakfast before going home for the weekend.

CHAPTER NINETEEN

Interviews

A FTER THE RELAXING TIME AT the private game reserve, Detective Sidd and Josh were back at Carter & Associates and continued to review all the files and photographs from the search and seizure operation as well as all information that had come up in the investigation. The only outstanding items were the memory cards, which were all encrypted, including the one from the office phone that they were most interested in.

They built up a list of interested persons to interview, each of who could possibly add further insight into who Wikus Louw really was and how he conducted his business. The list comprised neighbours, ex-business partners, community members and friends. Many of them had, like Josh's father, lost millions in retirement funds because of the Hillstrong share collapse. Some of them had had to sell holiday homes and cars, which forced them to live a much more conservative retirement life than that to which they had worked towards.

Josh and Detective Sidd were both hoping that this would be an aggravating factor towards Wikus Louw and be a reason why the interviewees would spill as much as possible about him.

They were in Detective Sidd's cruiser, driving at a leisurely pace; a bit too leisurely for Josh's taste. He and Detective Sidd had become close friends since the commencement of the investigation, but even still Josh did not feel it was at the stage where he could ask Detective Sidd if he would let Josh drive his car to speed things up a bit. Josh took the time instead to go through the files on the persons of interest while sitting shotgun.

They entered a wealthy golf estate on the outskirts of Johannesburg to commence their interview process with Wikus Louw's neighbour, Ms van Zyl, twice divorced and living very comfortably in her double-storey mansion. Her second husband was one of Wikus Louw's admirers and business associates who had drank whiskey and smoked cigars every chance he could with the business people that Wikus Louw entertained. That was the description of Ms van Zyl in the file that an officer had compiled about her. Josh and Detective Sidd were about to hear her version first hand. They pulled up to her home and knocked on the door.

"Josephina, there is someone at the door!" an elderly lady screamed. "Josephina! Oh, why do I even bother?" The door opened and Ms van Zyl changed her tone almost immediately. "Well, hello gentlemen, to what do I owe this pleasure today?" she said in an overly friendly manner. One could mistake her as being a bit flirtatious. She eyed Josh up and down and put out her hand for him to kiss. He shook it politely. Detective Sidd gave a quiet snort that only Josh could hear.

"My name is Josh Carter, I am a lawyer and this is Detective Sidd, we were hoping..."

"A detective and a lawyer at my house. What a lucky lady I am," she interrupted Josh and seemed to be going red in the face. She started fanning herself with a magazine she was holding.

"You young men are easy on the eyes too, if I may say so. Please come in, I would love the company." She led the two men inside and shouted again at her help. "Josephina! Damnit, where is she?"

and around the corner walked a Hispanic woman who answered the call of her employer.

"Sorry, Mrs van Zyl. I was up on the second floor, I came as soon as I could," she said out of breath.

"Yes, yes, it's alright. I welcomed these two gentlemen in myself, and for the last time please don't call me Mrs, I'm divorced, you know." She gave Josh a wink. "I would like another margarita and they will have whiskeys on the rocks, I assume?" she said, looking at them but not waiting for an answer. That would explain her forwardness: the margarita she was asking for was most definitely not the second one of the day.

Detective Sidd finally stepped in. "Ma'am, we are on official investigative business and we can't..."

"Nonsense, I won't tell if you don't. Josephina, two whiskeys and a margarita and we will have them by the pool." She kept walking towards large double glass doors leading outside. The house had large porcelain-white tiles, glass chandeliers and artwork covering the walls. The two men regarded each other for a moment and then followed suit.

Detective Sidd whispered to Josh, "I'm a married man. You will have to take one for the team, for the sake of our investigation," and he gave a soft laugh. Josh shook his head and smiled. This was going to be a very interesting day.

The entertainment area by the pool was large and open plan. The sparkling, crystal clear water was glistening in the sun and the lawn was neatly trimmed and regularly watered despite the water restrictions in place in the area. There were six deck chairs with thick cushions under large umbrellas. Inside the house the whining sound of a machine crushing ice could be heard. That was obviously Josephina making Ms van Zyl her fourth or fifth margarita for the day, even though it was only lunchtime.

The flirtatious elderly lady made herself comfortable and instructed the two men to do the same. "So," she began, "is this about that chauvinistic pig next door, or the one I used to be married to?" She had obviously had her fair share of bad men in her life; that much was clear already.

Josh was the one who answered this time. "Ms van Zyl, we would like to speak to you about Wikus Louw, your neighbour, and your ex-husband as well. We would like to know anything you can tell us about him that might help us understand what kind of man he is."

Josh had barely finished speaking when her monologue began. Detective Sidd took out his notebook and prepared himself to write down the key facts he thought were worth writing down, which weren't going to be many.

"Let me tell you about Wikus. He led me on for months. Whenever I went over there with my husband he would be so polite and complimentary and invite me over and then when I divorced my husband the invites stopped. He and his band of brothers, who drink and smoke cigars all night, talking about women like they're nothing but toys, are like school boys congratulating each other on the same damn rugby game.

"He would regularly host dinner parties. The spreads were divine obviously, only the best; he didn't spare a cent. He would have caterers and bartenders and live jazz bands for the evening dining, whereafter he and the other men would retreat to his man-cave while the women were left to socialise and ultimately find their own way home.

"Living next door was convenient for me. Oftentimes I would invite the ladies over and we would have a little party of our own. But one night the ladies were all going home and I decided to stay a little later on my own and eavesdrop on what those pigs were talking about. They're a bunch of criminals wearing suits and fancy watches, if you ask me."

She looked around and started to call out, "Joseph… Oh here you are. I was wondering where our drinks were." Josephina set the drinks down next to each person. You barely knew she was there. "And bring us a cheese board with biscuits, Josephina. These men look hungry!"

Josh didn't want to lose momentum. "We're fine thanks, Ms van Zyl, please don't worry about us," he tried, but Ms van Zyl wouldn't take no for an answer.

"Nonsense! What's a gathering without drinks and snacks, especially with young men that came all this way just to see little old me," she said, flattering herself.

Josh was eager to pick up the story again. "You said they were criminals, Ms van Zyl, what made you say that?"

"Yes, criminals!" She was back on track again. "One night I decided to stay late and listen in on their conversations. They were telling stories about their wives and their girlfriends whom their wives did not know about, and how much money they would make. Disgusting and childish. Wikus was the worst of them all. How he bragged about the way he treated his girlfriends on the side and the money that he blew on betting and gambling. Strip clubs, picking up girls at parties, and making the women crawl on their knees to fetch some money from themselves, making them beg; really demeaning things.

"But the other men idolised him, were trying to show off and impress him. It was pathetic to watch how the men would try to be like him, and of course they didn't have the same money as he did so they couldn't keep up. Many men spent money they didn't have just to be in his presence and hear promises of riches never to be theirs."

Josephina was back and placed the cheese board between the three of them. Josh nursed his whiskey. Detective Sidd was doing the same.

"Ms van Zyl, you called them criminals earlier. Did you hear or witness anything that was untoward? Something that may have made you suspicious about what your husband was doing with

Wikus Louw?" Josh brought the story back again. He stood up to help himself to a slice of brie and crackers, trying to act casual.

"You can't even reach the platter from there. Come and sit next to me. You'll be much more comfortable," she said, taking a large sip of her margarita and patting the cushion next to herself. Josh quickly looked at Detective Sidd while she was making space for him and saw that Detective Sidd mimed the words, "Take one for the team" with a huge grin on his face and a subtle thumbs up. He was enjoying this way too much.

Josh reluctantly sat next to Ms van Zyl, who wasted no time in putting her arm around him and then continued the story.

"Where was I now? Oh yes, criminals! I'm getting to that. I was listening in on one of their conversations. My ex-husband," she emphasised, "and two others were in that man-cave of Wikus's. He was trying to persuade all of them to buy shares in Hillstrong Holdings as usual. This time he said that there was a large merger imminent and that they could make a killing. I remember hearing one of the men saying he was very scared of being caught for knowing the information before it was officially released, but Wikus brushed it off, saying that no one would ever know and that it would all be done through companies that wouldn't be traced back to them. He said they should put everything they had into it, even take out mortgages on their homes if they had to, because it would be well worth it. He described it as an opportunity of a lifetime."

She paused the story to take a large sip of her margarita, almost emptying the glass. "Oh dear, I've run all out. Josephina!" and without waiting to be asked for another, Josephina was back and handing Ms van Zyl another refill.

"Ms van Zyl, can you remember the name of the companies and the merger details at all?" Josh asked, while Detective Sidd took detailed notes and sipped his whiskey.

"Oh no, dear. All that business talk was boring. I just made sure that my ex-husband couldn't take out another mortgage because when we got this house I kicked up a fuss that he would put it in my name and lucky I did! Where would I be now? Just like him in his two-bedroom house in the city. After all the women and drinking I eventually had enough, and then I divorced him," she said, not even bitterly, but quite proud of herself.

Josh and Detective Sidd gave each other a look to leave. They were not gaining much insight into Wikus Louw's character that they hadn't already heard, although Ms van Zyl had confirmed that insider trading was clearly a regular practice. Josh was a bit more eager to leave than his partner, and for good reason.

"Ms Van Zyl, you have been so very helpful, thank you for your time."

She was most disappointed that the two handsome men had to leave so quickly that they hadn't even finished their whiskey.

Detective Sidd and Josh left their first interviewee and got back on the road. Their next interview was about thirty minutes' drive from the margarita-loving lady. This was Mr Bernard James – two first names; his parents weren't that creative, and he obviously wasn't creative enough either otherwise he wouldn't be in the position that he was in now. He lived in a more modest home to that of Ms Van Zyl, although it hadn't always been like that. He'd probably landed up more like her husband. He'd used to live the high-life with his mates. He was fortunate enough to have other investments that he had not raided yet to purchase more and more shares in Hillstrong.

He'd agreed to talk to Detective Sidd and Josh as long as they assured him it was going to stay anonymous. He had lost a small fortune in the Hillstrong collapse; not as much as many people he knew, but enough. He knew many of his business associates and friends had worse things to worry about, criminal charges and the like.

He'd taken the loss quite well, Josh thought. He spoke about all investors taking a risk with any investment and that when it feels too good to be true it generally was and this case was no different. He said he'd suspected deep inside that what he was putting his money into wasn't a legitimate business. As much as he couldn't prove any foul play, the returns were just too great and the people whom he met who had the amount of money that was thrown around was just a red flag from the beginning.

"Mr James, we were wondering if you could explain your interactions with Wikus Louw, to help us understand what type of man he is. We know that you spent a reasonable amount of time with him throughout the years of Hillstrong's prime growth," Josh said.

"Despite how amazing he was at business and getting people to do what he wanted, he was quite unimaginative," said Bernard James. "I mean, knowing him from his younger years, as I did, I actually went to school with him. He never lived his own life; he wanted the lives of everyone around him who people admired. Instead of building a legacy of his own, he wanted to take over everybody else's. I'm sure you will know that the house he currently lives in once belonged to one of the wealthiest and best respected businessmen of South Africa. That is a clear example of what he would do. He had enough money to build the house of his dreams, but he wanted that one. Overpaid for it too! Made an offer nobody would refuse."

"What else did he buy that other people he admired owned?" Josh pushed further.

"Cars, horses, artwork on auction. He would outbid his competitors for pieces that he didn't even want, just because he could. It got really ugly in the race horse business too. He would buy the top three horses in their categories to eliminate any competition. The amount of money that he would spend was sinful.

"He set out to work for wealthy people and then made it his goal to one day overthrow the board and encourage hostile takeovers, and he used dirty tactics too. He would provide members of the board with kickbacks and expensive gifts which they always accepted, living the high life, and if they did not vote along with him then he would expose them.

"He even went as far as to have the men seduced by woman and cheat on their wives after they had drunk too much. He had cameras planted in the rooms. I heard that he would have photographs sent to the men's home address in manila envelopes just to ensure their loyalty stayed with him. It's like the Russians would do to their political members for extortion. People admired his ability to do business, but they feared him more than that. Sometimes people would want him to do business with them and give him a piece of the pie just so that he did not compete against them."

"Were you aware of any illegal dealings that Mr Louw took part in, insider trading? As a shareholder of Hillstrong, did you attend the annual meetings and request financials as part of your investment?" Josh enquired.

"No, nobody did. Once or twice a lone shareholder would stand up and make a comment about a lack of transparency and he would be annihilated by verbal abuse from Wikus. He spoke about trusting the executive and management team of the company and would say that if the shareholder wasn't satisfied with his returns he should sell his shares as Hillstrong didn't need any disloyal shareholders. The beaten shareholder would be reminded how much money Wikus' team made him.

"When Wikus said the word 'team' he generally meant himself. I'm not sure all of the executives or management even knew what he was up to with all the deals of Hillstrong. There were so many deals each year and the short amount of time that it took for approval for the transactions meant that they couldn't have gone through all the checks and balances.

"You must understand: Wikus is a business genius. He was so high on success nobody ever thought he could fail. Everyone who invested saw more returns in a few months than they'd had in years with all their investments combined. Wikus made the dream life a reality for people who'd thought they wouldn't see that type of money in their lifetime.

"Everyone wanted to be best friends with Wikus, and they were loyal too. He could ask them to do anything for him and it would get done. Nobody questioned him: not the board of Hillstrong, and for so many years not the auditors either or even international business people. He had such a far reach worldwide. It was incredible to see how this Afrikaans boy from humble beginnings grew such a great empire.

"I did hear that he once made an enemy, about twelve or thirteen years ago, with an Asian fellow, Chinese or Japanese, I never remember which one. A business deal went south, the negotiations did not turn out the way Wikus expected and the Asian guy pulled out and I remember the share price even fell. If you look at the track record of Hillstrong over the last decade and that will hardly appear as a blip on the radar, but at the time, when Wikus was still growing the group of companies, it was a big deal.

"Wikus was furious. He is a scary character when he is mad. He was embarrassed by the deal failing and he reported to a much stricter board back then. Well, that didn't seem to slow him down at all. Look what he did in the many years after that – increased his group of companies' reach across all borders."

Bernard James resigned himself to the fact that he too was fooled along with many other people. He had enjoyed the train ride for as long as he was on it but he had gotten off at the station short of his destination and would have to walk the rest of the way. Josh made a mental note of the Asian reference and watched Detective Sidd also write a note.

The investigator and the lawyer thanked their second interviewee for his time and made their way home. They discussed all the facts that they had been given and laughed some more about Ms Van Zyl eyeing out Josh like a high-school girl. Detective Sidd said he was definitely going to tell Gabby to watch out for competition.

CHAPTER TWENTY

Airport Arrest

JOSH WAS AT THE GYM. He had not seen the two large thugs again since noticing the tattoo on the man's forearm at the gym. He had made enquiries at the front desk regarding their identities but came up empty handed with video footage due to scheduled maintenance and their reluctance to hand over the personal information of their clients. He was waiting for a court order to assist with that.

He was holding a barbell with weights above his head when he felt his phone vibrating in his pocket. He pushed for two more reps of shoulder press before dropping it to the ground. He reached for his phone and saw the incoming call was from Detective Sidd so he answered immediately.

"Morning," he said breathlessly.

"Did I catch you at a bad time? Why are you breathing so heavily?" Sidd asked.

"Not at all, just at the gym. I was mid rep when you called. What's up?"

"We caught your boy Nicholas Webster and his secretary at the airport last night, trying to flee the country with fake passports.

Doesn't sound like the actions of an innocent man to me," Detective Sidd stated.

"Has he been questioned at all? Can I talk to him?" Josh asked, his heart racing now.

"I've arranged that you sit with him for an hour or so before he gets booked in. I've brought Rhonda in on it so that she can prosecute. Allows us more control to squeeze information out of him. Because your father is claiming that he lost money while invested in Hillstrong Holdings, Rhonda was able to justify that it falls within our investigation. Only condition is I have to be in the room when you talk to him, just a precaution due to the personal family interest, you know. We generally don't allow this sort of thing, but it is only in your capacity as commercial lawyer. You need to be on your best behaviour or else it could backfire on both of us. We're holding them at Randburg station. Meet me there when you're ready."

"Thanks, Mark. I really appreciate it. I'm going to take a shower and grab my files and I'll meet you at the station in an hour," said Josh.

"Great, see you then. I'll soften them up a bit and let them know how much trouble they are in," Detective Sidd said, chuckling to himself before he ended the call. This was obviously one of the things that Detective Sidd enjoyed about his job.

Josh thought about the interview they'd had with Ms van Zyl and how much Detective Sidd had enjoyed that, at Josh's expense. He jumped into the shower at the gym, his adrenalin pumping. Finally he would make some progress with his parent's investment funds. Over the past few weeks he had been going through the files of the other investors who had trusted Nicholas Webster with their money and had spoken with a few of them. In total, there were about ten people – not a large investment group, but with the fees that Nicholas was charging and the amounts of money that he was skimming off the top of each of his client's accounts, he was making a hefty margin.

Most of the investors to whom Josh had spoken had had the same reaction as his parents – they had not authorised any investment more than a certain percentage of their funds into a high risk investment pool, no more than thirty percent of the investment funds, but in most cases Nicholas had invested up to ninety percent in Hillstrong Holdings.

Josh had raised the possibility of a class action suit and asked whether the investors would be interested in joining, and it was unanimous: they would do anything they could to recoup their lifetime's savings. All of the investors to whom Josh had spoken to were over the age of fifty-eight, which meant that the money they'd lost was supposed to be their nest egg for their retirement. That was now gone.

One of the investor's wives had told Josh that her husband had died of a heart attack from the shock of the news that his retirement savings had been lost to the market. If it weren't for her husband's life insurance that paid out, she wouldn't be able to survive on the government grants available to her, and now she would be spending her retirement alone, without her husband. This was part of what motivated Josh to bring justice to this greedy man.

He had offered to take on the class action suit on a contingency fee basis, meaning that he would be working for no charge unless they won, and he said that if the judge awarded his costs then he would recoup that from Nicholas Webster and would not charge any of the investors any fees. He remembered how he had been fuelled by helping Vivian claim from the Workers Compensation Fund. Although nothing could compensate the loss that someone experienced from losing a loved one, a court outcome, especially a victorious one, brought a small sense of closure to the victims. It helped them move on with their mourning phase, feeling like they had done everything they could in the unjust situation that they were going through.

He was showered, dressed and on his way to the station, his meeting binder on the passenger seat of his BMW. After all his own investigating and reviewing of the investor's files, he had constructed his case against Nicholas Webster already, in the hope that they would catch him, and now they had.

He arrived at the Randburg Police Station, grabbed his meeting binder and the two takeaway coffees he had picked up from Starbucks on the way. Detective Sidd deserved the roasted bean treat. The lady at the reception desk was waiting for Josh and immediately let him through security to Detective Sidd's office.

"Morning Mark, I brought coffee," said Josh. Detective Sidd was on the phone, his desk covered with papers.

He ended the call and greeted Josh. "Ah, just what I needed, thank you." He took the coffee from Josh and breathed in the aroma of the steaming coffee while closing his eyes. He took a sip and enjoyed every sensation of the coffee in his hand.

"Alright. Now that I am caffeinated, let's talk about our boy. Turns out the passport was real; his real name is Nicholas Nel. He has been using a fake name for business and to evade paying his wife and child maintenance. He was initially playing hardball and thought that all we could pin on him was the fake name. He said it was to prevent his ex-wife from finding him. So we told him the consequences of not paying child and spousal maintenance and he started negotiating.

"Once I mentioned your name he realised that we had him on the hook for it all, the whole lot. He must have gone ten shades whiter before asking for his lawyer. This was about fifteen minutes ago. You can have an hour with him and then we are obligated to call his lawyer; you know the routine. Tell him we couldn't reach his lawyer but we will keep trying. And make sure he consents to the interrogation while his lawyer isn't in the room. We will be filming the whole time.

"I don't need to say anything more to you. Josh, I realise you have a personal stake in this for your parents' sake, so tell me I'm not making a big mistake letting you go in there. You have to have it under control, understand?"

"Don't worry, Mark, I will be on my best behaviour, my best lawyer behaviour. This is strictly business. You can trust me. I know that you have gone out on a limb for me and I assure you I will be able to restrain myself from reaching over the table and slapping him," he said with a smile.

"Here we go," said Detective Sidd with a sigh, not sure whether he was taking an unnecessary risk or whether Josh would be able to resist the temptation. "Let's go, time is running out. Mandy is in the room next door to his. Surprisingly, she hasn't said a word yet. She wanted her lawyer immediately. She is handling this a bit smarter than he is. I wouldn't be surprised if she turns on him. You can use that when speaking to Nicholas."

Josh and Detective Sidd entered the interrogation room. Nicholas took one look at Josh and dropped his head in defeat. Josh reached onto the table and switched the microphone on and began. "Nicholas Webster, or should I say Nicholas Nel? We were unable to reach your lawyer but we have staff trying continuously and I'm sure he will be here soon. May I speak with you for a short while? I guarantee you will want to hear what I have to say."

Nicholas looked at Josh and then at Detective Sidd, said nothing, and nodded.

"Mr Nel, I need you to verbally answer for the record," Josh gestured towards the red light on the microphone on the table.

"Yes," he said, his voice sounding croaky and stressed.

"I understand from Detective Sidd here that he has mentioned that you are likely to be charged with evading your legal obligations of child and spousal maintenance; that along with the fake name is already a criminal offence, offering, how much, Mark? Five to ten years?"

"Something like that, Mr Carter. I think we could motivate a case for ten. Judges don't like men who run away from their family responsibilities," added Detective Sidd while staring at Nicholas. They were playing bad cop, bad cop. There was to be no break for Nicholas Nel today.

Josh continued. "I want to talk to you about your business, Mr Nel. We performed a search and seizure operation on your apartment and your offices and confiscated all of your files. My father's file, as well as all of your other clients' files, contained a similar document." Josh removed the consent form from his meeting binder which allowed funds to be invested into Hillstrong Holdings. "None of your client's recognised this form. You forged it so that you could take a higher percentage of fees and you didn't think Hillstrong Holding's shares would ever drop in value."

Nicholas Nel stared down at the table and said nothing.

"Mr Nel, I have been requested by your clients to institute a class action against you. In total you owe over R100 million to your clients. I want to offer you a settlement proposal, one that allows you to stay out of court in respect of the investment charges. If you settle out of court on this matter then a criminal charge for fraud can be left off the charge sheet. Now we understand from performing a lifestyle background check on you that you don't have the full R100 million, but you will come damn near close to it, and if your investments are in the right place, unlike your clients, you will be able to pay ninety cents on the Rand to your clients in the next six months. After all, the investments are all from funds that were saved and invested by the hard working retirees over a period of forty years," said Josh.

"Also, we have impounded the Ferrari you parked in long term parking at the airport. That will be sold at auction as well," said Detective Sidd.

Nicholas Nel looked as though he was going to be sick. His face was pale and he was shaking slightly. He did not answer Josh or Detective Sidd but instead asked for a cigarette while he waited for his lawyer. Josh and Detective Sidd left the interrogation room and found out that Nicholas Nel's lawyer had been contacted and would be there shortly.

"If I ever saw a man who was going to crack, that's him. We've got him!" said Detective Sidd.

"Let's hope so," said Josh. "While we wait let's go talk to Mandy."

The men walked to the interrogation viewing room and looked through the one-way glass. Mandy was speaking to her lawyer in private. The intercom system was switched off, as she was discussing her legal case and it was under attorney-client privilege. Mandy was speaking very animatedly to her lawyer who was trying to calm her down. Josh could just make out the words, "I can't go to jail! I'm way too pretty for jail." Now was the time to interrogate.

Josh and Detective Sidd knocked on the door and entered the interrogation room and were introduced to Mandy's lawyer, Randall Sloan.

"Detective Sidd, Mr Carter, my client has something to offer the State in exchange for providing information on Mr Webster," he said.

"Nel," Josh corrected him.

"Excuse me?"

"His name is Nicholas Nel, not Webster," Josh said.

This time it was Mandy who responded. "Are you kidding me? He lied to me about his name?"

"Don't say anything, Mandy, I will handle this," Randall Sloan said to his client. "As I was saying, my client has information on Mr Nel in exchange for immunity on the charges against her," he said with the best brave poker face he could muster as he knew the cards he was holding were not a very strong hand.

"Mr Randall, your client has been charged with corporate fraud, or being an accomplice in the alternative. To be exact, ten counts of fraud to the amount of R100 million. She was also found trying to leave the country, which makes her a flight risk. You know as well as I do that the threshold of R500 000 for a minimum sentence to be imposed was exceeded a while ago. In aggravation of that, the victims of the crime are elderly people who have lost their lifetime savings. One of Mr Nel's and Mandy's clients had a heart attack and died of the shock of his retirement funds being lost. That blame rests on Mr Nel and your client," said Josh.

Mandy was looking around anxiously. "Randall, what does that mean? Won't they make a deal? Randall I can't go to jail!" she said in a panic, tears rolling down her face.

Now Josh decided to deliver the final blow. "Mr Randall, the minimum sentence for a crime like this is fifteen years. She could be out and under house arrest after a few years, though."

Mandy's face lost all colour. She turned in her seat and vomited all over the interrogation floor. Detective Sidd, sitting opposite her, quickly moved his feet so that he didn't get any on his shoes.

Randall handed her a handkerchief he kept in his breast pocket of his suit. He tried again.

"Mr Carter, perhaps we could look at community service as well as a fine to be paid? My client may be able to source some funds to recoup the losses. My client denies knowledge of all of the clients of Mr Nel, and says that the reason she was leaving the country was because Mr Nel promised her a romantic getaway."

"Mr Sloan, we performed a lifestyle background check on your client and it is unlikely that she would be able to make a significant difference to recoup any losses that were experienced by the victims of Mr Nel's brokerage," said Josh.

"My dad," Mandy said quietly, staring at the floor.

"I beg your pardon?" said Josh

"My dad is a very wealthy man. He will pay you if you don't make me go to jail," she sobbed.

Josh wanted to investigate the extent of her father's wealth before committing to anything. Although he had every intention of making a deal with her, he wanted to make her sweat and offer everything to them, and it seemed she had just done so.

"Alright. We will consider your proposal and get back to you. I'll have two coffees sent in here for you two while you wait, and I'll get someone to clean that up," said Josh, gesturing to the vomit on the floor.

The two men left the room and went back to Nicholas Nel's interrogation room. His lawyer had now arrived, dressed much more elegantly than Mandy's lawyer. The fees were probably three times the amount as Randall's as well.

"Gentlemen," he greeted as they entered the room. "My name is Edward Grimes."

"Josh Carter and Detective Sidd," Josh answered and he began immediately with the charges against Nicholas Nel to determine what his lawyer was able to wangle. "Mr Grimes, you will have seen the charge sheet, that Mr Nel has been accused of ten counts of fraud to the value of R100 million. The minimum sentence proposed by the prosecution would be at least fifteen years, if not more. An aggravating factor would be that the victims of his crime are vulnerable, elderly people who trusted him with their money.

"As we told your client's receptionist, Mandy, one of your clients had a heart attack from the shock of losing all his money. He is now dead. His wife will be spending her retirement years alone. That will be placed on your client as well.

"In addition to these charges, your client has also breached a court order for child and spousal maintenance and using a fake identity and, since he was attempting to flee the jurisdiction of the court, he is now deemed a flight risk."

"Mr Carter, my client has informed me that you proposed an out of court settlement at least for the funds that were lost. My client, without admitting any liability whatsoever, has made a few mistakes and has been running a legitimate financial advisory business and deserves to be compensated for his work. The sum claimed of R10 million would completely bankrupt my client and leave him destitute. I have advised him to accept a deal depending on the terms of the settlement. We could make an arrangement for half of the claim."

Josh's ears were burning with anger. He turned to Detective Sidd. "Mark, did he say he deserves to be compensated?" Detective Sidd shifted uneasily in his chair.

"Mr Grimes, please don't think that your argument is going to fly in a court of law," said Josh, his voice slightly shaky with rage. "A man died from the shock of losing his lifetime savings, your client preyed on the elderly and fraudulently invested their money where he had no right to! Do not tell me about what he deserves!" Josh was raising his voice now.

"Mr Carter, it appears that you are taking this matter personally because of one of my clients is your father. Perhaps you are not the appropriate person for the negotiations," Grimes said.

Josh got up from his chair suddenly, which even gave Detective Sidd a fright, and leaned over the table glaring at Mr Grimes. He spoke softly to Detective Sidd without breaking eye contact with Mr Grimes. "Mark, I think we will have better luck going to trial with Mr Nel. I believe we can have him sentenced to fifteen years and ordered to pay a fine of R100 million as well. The judges do not take these crimes very lightly. That would solve all of his problems because, if he is in prison for so long, he won't need any money of his own."

Josh's tone was calm with the edge of being pushed over the edge. It was terrifying. He stood up straight. "It seems our business is done here. The deal is off the table," he said and turned to leave.

Detective Sidd rose from his chair and was following Josh to leave the room when Nicholas Nel called out, "Stop! Wait, I will accept your deal! I'll sign it, for the R90 million out-of-court settlement! Please don't retract the deal!"

"Very well. The prosecutor's office will let you have a draft agreement for your consideration by the end of the day. When your consultation is over, you will be taken to the holding cells. I trust that Mr Grimes informed you that, given your evasion of paying spouse and child maintenance, you will be deemed a flight risk and you are unlikely to be granted bail. Your first appearance for that matter will be tomorrow and you will find out," Josh said to him.

Nicholas said nothing but nodded in defeat. The two men left the interrogation room. Detective Sidd closed the door behind them to find Josh grinning from ear to ear.

"Josh, were you just –"

"– yip, I thought you would have picked up on the whole bad cop routine?" he said laughing.

Detective Sidd held his chest and exhaled deeply, "Next time warn me, man, I almost had a heart attack, I could just picture you reaching across the table and slapping Nel's lawyer." Then, after relaxing a little bit, he gave a laugh himself. "Did you see their faces?"

"Thank you, Mark. Your assistance in this matter has been extremely helpful," Josh said.

"Only a pleasure, Josh, glad I could help. I'll speak to the guys in Rhonda's office and have the settlement agreement drawn up. I'll also look at how much Mandy's father is worth. Maybe we can make up any shortfall there. I'll let you know."

"Thanks, I'm going back to the office to do some work. Speak to you later," said Josh.

CHAPTER TWENTY-ONE

Personal Companies

SITTING IN THE WAR ROOM at the offices of Carter & Associates, Josh and Detective Sidd were pouring over the investigation documents. Josh had concluded his review of all of the email correspondence. Unfortunately, there were no further leads to what had really happened between Hillstrong Holdings and Hung Industries. Without the actual findings of Hung Industries, it would be difficult to know any more. The news clippings from the time of the negotiations were varied and unreliable: feuds between the two CEOs, the purchase price not being enough, and then wild accusations that both of the men had unreasonable requirements for the fulfilment of the transaction that the other wouldn't agree to.

He still couldn't figure out why the conversation at the Ranch House had been cut short, and whether there really was something that Fei Hung had to attend to, or whether Simon Chen had created that excuse to end the line of questioning.

Then, suddenly, Josh found something of high interest. "Mark, this file you seized at Wikus' home office is a recordal of transactions that were concluded between a variety of companies all held either solely or partly by the Louw Family Trust. The only beneficiaries are our guy Wikus, his wife and his children. The file has three main sub-categories with the name of three companies: they are PropCo (Pty) Ltd, InvestCo (Pty) Ltd, and RaceCo (Pty) Ltd. The first appears to be a property holding company, the second an investment and securities holding company, and the last one is solely dedicated to horse breeding and racing. I'm briefly looking at the RaceCo company financials that he has here. Do you have any idea how much race horses cost?" Josh added, "He has spent hundreds of millions on acquiring, grooming and racing these horses."

"Sounds like a lucky break for us! And I have good news. I have just received a text from the IT technician team. Our memory cards are ready and they were able to decrypt the recordings on the phone as well as all the data on the memory cards we found in the walk-in safe. I'm going back to the station to get those and to fill Rhonda in on our progress.

"I also have to go finalise the plea agreements for Nicholas and Mandy. Her father was willing to pay a fine on her behalf to the amount of twenty million, and he was more than happy to let his daughter do a thousand hours of community service to teach her a lesson as well. That amount will cover fees as well."

"That's great news. Let me know when the paperwork is concluded so that I can inform my parents there's a chance most of their retirement savings could possibly be returned," said Josh, relieved at the outcome.

"Will do. Be in touch," Detective Sidd said and left the War Room.

Josh had the task of performing a thorough analysis on each of the three private companies. This meant knowing exactly who all the directors and shareholders are, what deals the entities concluded, and with which other companies. He already knew the transactions would not be at arm's length, meaning between two unrelated and independent parties. Wikus would have a personal interest in both parties.

He read through the documents meticulously, starting with the PropCo file. The amount of immovable property that had passed through this company was astonishing. According to the property reports, properties were purchased by the PropCo entity at what appeared to be market-related prices and later sold to Hillstrong Holdings for what was clearly an exorbitantly inflated amount.

Josh performed a company report on the three investment properties and was not surprised to find out who the sole director of all of them was: Wikus Louw. He would bet that either Wikus had not discloses the deals to the rest of the board of directors and shareholders at all, or that he had not disclosed his personal financial interest in any of the transactions, thereby breaching his fiduciary duty in terms of the Companies Act.

Shareholding was going to be more difficult to prove because in South Africa it was no longer a requirement to lodge the shareholding with the Companies and Intellectual Property Commission, only the directorships.

He looked over one of the sales for a residential property in an area of Johannesburg that was considered by all means middle class. The property was purchased by Wikus through PropCo at a price of R3.4million and was sold three years later for the impressive amount of R45 million to Hillstrong Holdings. There were more ludicrous figures. Sometimes the increase of the purchase price was as much as twelve hundred percent.

He continued his review of sale agreements and noticed that many of them were signed off by Hillstrong Holdings as the purchaser and by PropCo as the seller, with the same signature on both party signature lines. Wikus Louw had been dealing with himself on behalf of his personal property investment company and also as if Hillstrong Holdings was his own personal investment company.

It took Josh a couple of hours to finish reviewing all of the PropCo deals that had been filed. And then he struck gold with a shareholder's agreement. The agreement set out the rights of the shareholders of PropCo. Now he could see who the ultimate beneficiaries of all these profits were. The results surprised him. There was, of course, the Wikus Louw Family Trust as the majority shareholder, the family trust of the founder of Hillstrong Holdings, the Hillstrong Family Trust, and then there was a shareholder described in the agreement as a silent shareholder.

This portion of shares was held in a shelf company called for the benefit of FH Incorporated. It is clear that this company was created to act as an SPV, or Special Purpose Vehicle. The purpose of this "vehicle" was to hold the investment on behalf of someone who did not want their identity to be disclosed. Possibly for tax evasion reasons, or in this case to remove suspicion of irregular deals and possibly even money laundering.

Josh performed a company report search on the SPV company and FH Incorporated. There was a sole director who was a well-known lawyer at a law firm that specialised in incorporating company structures in jurisdictions globally. This was a problem because, as the director was also a lawyer and would be acting in terms of a mandate, he would be bound by attorney-client confidentiality and would not have to disclose the details of his client, the actual owner of the shares. The law firm would obviously receive a hefty fee for being the face of the company that held the shares in PropCo. Josh would have to do some further digging into that SPV and FH Incorporated.

He turned his attention to the InvestCo file that contained all the documents setting out the securities and financial investments held by it. He already knew that the sole director was again Wikus Louw. He went through various company reports, which showed just how many pies Wikus Louw had his fingers in.

Then Josh made a discovery that uncovered why the banks had instituted so many urgent applications against Wikus Louw in the High Court of South Africa. InvestCo, Hillstrong Holdings and multiple other companies had taken hundreds of millions of Rand in loans – and here was the terrifying part – using Hillstrong Holdings shares as collateral for the loans. When the share price dropped below the required debt cover ratio, the banks would call up the loans for repayment, but when the share price dropped ninety-five percent in only a few days, there was no loan repayment to call up. The house of cards collapsed and the banks would never get their money back.

This had been kept under the radar from the country and shareholders at large. Even though court cases were public record, Josh had not seen much news reporting on this. Josh found now that the magnitude of this corporate crash was worse than he'd ever expected. Again, the shelf company FH Incorporated, and the other shelf companies that were created, had all taken out loans from the bank. Josh did not understand how they'd managed to secure the loans without providing security. A bank could never grant a loan without security.

Then Josh found the document that answered this question: a cession and suretyship agreement on behalf of all of these companies, signed by a representative of Hillstrong Holdings to cover the debt in the event that the companies defaulted, and once again the security was Hillstrong shares. He recognised the signature on the last page as Wikus Louw's. Wikus Louw, using Hillstrong as his own personal finance company to transact with other companies that belonged to him, siphoning out money in staged transactions in which he was a related party with a personal financial interest. None of the financial statements, board, or shareholder minutes reflected any disclosures for any of these transactions.

CHAPTER TWENTY-TWO

Suicide

It was Saturday afternoon. Josh, Gabby and Daniel were walking around the neighbourhood park eating ice-cream in sugar cones. It was a beautiful summer day with many families spending their weekend on picnic blankets under beach umbrellas while their children ran around playing games. The park was hosting a family market day with food stalls and other tables ranging from home crafts to early Christmas decorations and gifts. Christmas was still a month and a half away, but it was never too early to begin the Christmas festivities. It was, after all, the best time of year for Josh and Gabby. They both loved Christmas time. Josh and Gabby had bought a family Christmas tree to put up and decorate on the first of December.

Gabby was taking the boys to view show houses that Josh was interested in and so they'd decided to make a day of it. They had viewed two houses earlier that Josh had found to be great options but felt still lacked some of his requirements – a triple garage, a home office, at least a splash pool, and enough space to create his Japanese garden. He had already drawn out the plans for the garden and knew how much excess space he needed. He wasn't in a rush to move, so they had time to look around and get exactly what he wanted. Gabby assured him she had left the best house of the day for last and she was sure he would like it more than the others.

Josh bought four used books from the second hand book table, not knowing when he would have time to read them, but he had to feed his addiction for buying books. He would add them to the shelf at home until he had some time off. He usually read a few over the December holiday, when he actually took a break from his law firm. Hopefully this year was going to be different. He would conclude his investigation into Hillstrong Holdings and then take a decent holiday with Gabby and Daniel. They had already decided they would go to the coast for some sea, sun and surf. Daniel had only been to the beach when he was a baby and so he couldn't remember what it was like; he was beyond excited to go.

They arrived at the last house of the day. It was situated on a hill and boasted beautiful views of the city from the back side of the house, similar to what Carter & Associates offered. It met all the requirements on Josh's list. The wide driveway to the double-storey home ended in a triple garage that led into the main entrance of the house. The kitchen, dining room, and entertainment area were all laid out in a modern open-plan and opened onto an outside patio and braai area.

He looked out onto the yard. There was enough space for his Japanese garden, with a lengthy narrow pool to swim laps and a beautiful deck finish around the water's edge. He envisioned the rock fountain and Japanese landscaping plans that he'd drawn out would fit the outside area perfectly.

Gabby watched him closely the whole time, not saying anything except pointing out one or two features that she thought he would be happy with. Upstairs housed all the bedrooms, three of them with en-suite bathrooms and an extra one perfectly situated for Josh to make his office. The view from that second floor room would look over the Japanese garden that he would create and also have a view of the city many kilometres away.

The main room was next to the office and had glass sliding doors that opened onto a balcony overlooking the same view as the would-be home office. Because of the slant of the hill upon which the house was built, it was unlikely that anyone would be looking into his house. All the homes in that area faced in the direction of the city, away from the hill. As an added bonus that excited Gabby about the house, there was a walk-in closet the size of an additional room that already had a layout for all of his suits. The other two bedrooms were similar in design and had smart finishes. If all his plans came to fruition he wondered which of the two Daniel would choose.

The house was incredible.

"So?" Gabby said, not able to contain herself any longer.

"It's perfect, Gabs. It has everything I'm looking for and more," he said.

"Really? That's great, I was so sure you were going to love it! The other two houses were just a warm up for this one, a strategy I use when I think I've found the one!" She smiled mischievously at him.

"Well, I mean, I think it's the one, not entirely set on it yet, I just need some confirmation first," he said with a serious face.

Gabby's face couldn't hide her disappointment. "What is it? The price is slightly higher than what you stated, but within reason, and I'm sure I can talk the seller down a bit!" she said eagerly.

"No, that's not it," he said and walked out onto the main bedroom's balcony to watch Daniel running around the garden with a toy aeroplane. Gabby followed.

"What aren't you sure about, Josh?" she asked anxiously.

"Whether it is the perfect home..." he said, paused and then finished his line, "...for the three of us." He looked at her lovingly and her eyes immediately welled up with tears and she attempted a smile. He pulled her closer. "Gabs, the past year has been amazing with you and Daniel staying with me and I don't want it to change after the investigation. I was hoping you would consider moving in with me when I buy this house." Now he felt like the anxious one.

"Yes, we would love that, Josh!" She hugged him. They kissed in the summer breeze as the sun set; they were going to share many sunsets on that balcony.

She called her little boy from above while waving to him. "Dan, do you like the house?"

"It's so great, Mom. You did good!" he said to his mother. And then to Josh, "You should really buy it!" He looked up at the two adults standing together on the balcony, holding each other.

"You tell him," Gabby said to Josh.

"I like it too, bud. I think I'm going to buy it! But only on one condition," he said.

"What is it?" Daniel asked.

"I'll only buy it if you and your mom come live with me in it."

Daniel's face lit up. "For real? You mean this will be our house too, and we will all live together?" he shouted, and looked around with new eyes, full of possibility.

"That's right, bud. So what do you say? Shall we take it?"

"That would be so awesome!" Daniel ran under the balcony into the house. The quick succession of thud thud thud thud of his feet on the stairs could be heard until he entered the main room and walked out onto the balcony where Josh and Gabby stood. He was breathing heavily but did not stop until he ran into their arms and hugged them.

Gabby's eyes teared up again. She caught Josh's gaze and whispered, "Thank you".

"Shall we go out and celebrate?" he asked.

"Let's go to Isabelle's!" said Gabby.

"Perfect," Josh said as his phone rang. The caller ID showed Detective Sidd.

"Mark, hi."

"Josh, I have some bad news. Our boy Nicholas Nel is dead. He hanged himself in his holding cell with the legs of his pants."

"Shit." Josh walked away so that Daniel wouldn't hear the conversation. "What about the plea agreement, did he sign it?"

"It doesn't seem like it, Josh. I asked the officer on duty and she said that she was instructed to go fetch him to take him to the interrogation room to see his lawyer and then she found him like that. She called for help immediately but he had been dead for a while. Who knows how long he was hanging there."

Josh sighed deeply. "But we have him on the recorder agreeing to the settlement. That has to be worth something. Thanks for letting me know, Mark. What about Mandy? Did she sign her settlement with the State, for the R20 million?" he asked.

"Yes, that has just been signed, although that only gives investors about twenty cents on the rand for their claims after the fees are paid," said Detective Sidd.

"I know. It's not much at all once you divide it all up, but it's something," said Josh, disappointed. "Thanks, Mark. See you tomorrow in the War Room?"

"See you there, Josh. I'm sorry about this. I know this has been hard on you and your parents."

"Thanks, Mark. See you tomorrow." He ended the call. He was disappointed that his parents' fight for their money would now prove more difficult. He took a moment to reflect that someone had ended their life because of this mess. Money could cause so many problems.

Josh relayed the conversation to Gabby who shared in the disappointment. "Is there something you need to do at the office or with Mark? If you need to go work you really can!" she said.

"No, there's nothing for me to do right now, nothing I can't take care of tomorrow. Let me just give my parents a call and give them the news, then we are going to go celebrate the fact that my personal real estate agent found us a house! This will not ruin our day," he said and smiled at her.

"Great, I'll phone the seller and tell her I found a buyer!" she replied.

Josh walked around his soon-to-be home and called his parents' house. His mother answered and Josh could hear the disappointment in her voice. It broke Josh inside. His mother thanked him for everything and said at least they would be getting something.

Josh knew that his parent's retirement life would be vastly different to what they had worked so hard for all their life. They would have to downsize the house, sell the race-car and live as conservatively as possible because every expense was a leak of finances and there was no more income into the household.

He went and found Gabby in the kitchen downstairs waiting with Daniel to go to Isabelle's.

CHAPTER TWENTY-THREE

Disturbing Calls

JOSH AND DETECTIVE SIDD WERE in the War Room at Carter & Associates early on Monday morning, Josh nursing a slight hangover from the bottle of red wine that he and Gabby had shared the previous night at Isabelle's. He and Detective Sidd wanted an early start to the day because they had received the recordings from Wikus Louw's home office phone.

The IT technicians had given a description on the workings of the phone recording system and stated that all of the calls that were made from the office phone should have been recorded as well as any calls forwarded to a mobile phone, and the files that were uploaded contained specific time stamps for each call.

Josh looked at the list of calls. Wikus Louw had not made use of the office line very much. He supposed that with cell phones being so prevalent it was actually unusual to have a land line.

The boardroom was looking messier than ever before, which was a good sign in all investigations. The two white-boards were filling up with pictures of people of interest, and notes and leads were written next to them. There was a new section consisting of the three personal investment entities belonging to Wikus Louw and certain of his associates. Finally, Josh and Detective Sidd were able to bring in more of the Hillstrong Holdings directors and link them to actual transactions.

Initially, it had looked as if Wikus Louw had single-handedly implemented all of the transactions, which of course could not be the case. He would have probably negotiated the deals on his own and might even have kept certain details to himself, but he'd certainly required loyal and blind followers to carry out his instructions without question.

A failure to uphold a fiduciary duty to a company could also comprise not asking questions when a reasonable and diligent director would do so in the circumstances. Where there was insufficient clarity for any business deal, directors had a duty to report to shareholders and act responsibly with their investments.

The two men were seeking any piece of information that would enable them to charge the senior executives and directors of the boards of these related companies with something specific, something that clearly showed a breach of fiduciary duties.

They drew a box on the side of the white board representing an entity and labelled it FH Incorporated. It was the only entity they'd struggled to find any information on. It had shared in the profits of most of the side deals that Wikus had orchestrated with his personal investment companies and shelf entities. They looked up the call recordings on the secure server and selected a file with a date stamp only days before the news of Hillstrong's financial woes broke. Immediately upon listening to the first phone call they knew that they had uncovered a material part of the investigation.

They listened as Wikus sat at his desk early one morning after receiving a phone call from Karl Helmut, founder of Hillstrong Holdings.

"Wikus, where are you? We have a problem!" Helmut said quickly.

"Hi Karl, I am at my home. What is the matter?"

"The auditors are not willing to sign off the annual financial statements. They have requested a forensic investigation. I told them that I'm sure that won't be necessary, they must just talk to you and then you will answer any questions that they may have to clear it up," said Karl in an impatient and worried tone.

"Karl, what is the specific issue now? I have repeatedly answered their questions and provided them with documents on numerous occasions when they have requested them. Why are they battling to do their jobs? Our structure is a very complex one, but I have explained this to them," answered Wikus.

"I don't know, but please just talk to them. We have a few members of the board here trying to answer their questions but no one has the knowledge and the details of the transactions like you. I can put you on speaker now."

"Alright, yes fine, let me speak to them," Wikus said impatiently.

They heard the auditor's team leader on the phone, his voice shaking. "Mr Louw, unfortunately we cannot sign off the annual financial statements unless we receive certain vital supporting documentation."

Wikus Louw became angry and defensive. "I have given you everything that you need! Do I have to do your job as well as mine now? What are the issues that you have? Tell me!" he demanded.

"Mr Louw, in the balance sheet there are numerous concerns around many property deals. The valuations of the properties have increased excessively over the last year and we are concerned that they are overvalued by a large stretch. Furthermore, many of these deals..." he paused, as if nervous to continue.

"Many of these deals...what?" Wikus Louw demanded.

"Many of these deals appear to be related-party transactions, which in themselves may not be an issue, but Mr Louw there has been no disclosure to the board, shareholders or in the financial statements regarding this."

There was a moment's silence before Wikus Louw could be heard on the other end of the line. "And what else is there that worries you? Give me the list!"

"Mr Louw, there is also a line item including a sum of R800 million as profit for an acquisition of an overseas entity for which there are no supporting documents to confirm the transaction has been concluded," he quickly continued before being shouted at by Wikus Louw again about how incompetent he was at his job. "And lastly, Mr Louw, there is great concern around the cash and cash equivalents. There has been a large sum dedicated to money owing to the Hillstrong Group that we have no documentation for that has improved the balance sheets quite substantially but we are concerned that the true valuation of the group is substantially lower."

The room where the board members and auditors sat was silent before Karl Helmut spoke up. "Wikus, as you can hear, they are extremely concerned about a few serious issues but we know that you can clear it up for us. I think it may be best for you to come in to the office along with any documentation that you feel will clear up their concerns, otherwise they are demanding a forensic audit on our books," he said, politely, but anxiously.

"Yes, fine, I'll come in. I can already tell you that there is nothing to worry about. I am also certain that I have provided all the necessary documentation to them already. But in any event, I'll be there in two hours, just wait for me," he said, not quite as angry and impatient as before but his tone was still unpleasant.

"Thank you, Wikus, we will wait for you," said Karl Helmut and the call ended.

The next call's time-stamp showed a time two and a half hours later.

It was Karl Helmut again. "Wikus, are you still at home?" he said, more impatient than before, but still polite.

"No I am on my way. My home office line is forwarded to my cell. I'm in my Bentley, I'll be there soon. It took me longer than expected to compile all of the documents that are needed," he replied.

"Alright, but hurry. We need the auditors to review the documents and have them signed off so that we can release our financials on time, as announced to the public and the shareholders!" he expressed the urgency of the situation.

"I will be there as soon as possible," was all that Wikus Louw said before the call ended. Obviously Wikus Louw did not make that meeting because the next call from Karl Helmut was answered by Wikus and cut short after saying a mere three words, "I'm sorry, Karl". Over the next few hours, Karl Helmut made a further three calls to Wikus Louw, all of which went to Wikus Louw's voicemail.

Detective Sidd and Josh were grateful that the line was still being forwarded and recorded. The first two calls contained similar pleas to talk to him and come in to the office.

"Wikus, what is going on? Where are you? We are waiting for you! Just come in and talk to us; we can sort whatever it is out!"

It seemed as if the realisation of what must be happening set in with the members of the board and the auditors because the calls stopped for a period of time, and when they started again the tones of the callers were vastly different.

The last incoming call from Karl Helmut took place three hours after Wikus Louw had said he was already on his way. Karl pleaded with Wikus. "Whatever has happened is done. We just want you to help us fix this mess. This could destroy Hillstrong. Please come in and talk to us! The market will eat us alive!"

There were two other calls from members of the board who had merely phoned to check whether Wikus was alright.

The last call for the day was an outgoing call made by Wikus to Karl Helmut late in the evening. This time it was Karl who did not answer the line and it went to his voice mail. Wikus sounded drunk and emotional, his speech slurred. He could be heard tapping a bottle against a glass while pouring a drink and placing the bottle down on his wooden desk and taking sips in between speech.

"Karl, I've made so many mistakes. I'm so sorry for the embarrassment I have now caused for your company." It was ironic to hear Wikus refer to the company as someone else's when for the past many years he had been acting as though it were his own.

Wikus was sniffing and sobbing silently. "I will not be able to fix the financials in time for the release date. I have disappointed many people. So many people are going to lose money and I take full responsibility. Please know that nobody else in executive management is involved in any of this. I acted alone and I will face the consequences. Please continue to believe in the Hillstrong brand and pick up the pieces." Wikus was now sobbing uncontrollably and the phone dropped onto the desk with a loud thud before it was placed back on the receiver, ending the call.

Josh and Detective Sidd sat silently, trying to absorb all of the evidence that they had just heard.

"Well, that is probably going to be as close to a confession as we will ever get, unless he breaks down in the witness box," said Detective Sidd.

"I think so too. I have heard that he has lawyered up with a team of the best and is denying responsibility, which is completely contradictory to this vital evidence that we have just heard," said Josh.

"He may have a team of the best lawyers, but we have you!" said Detective Sidd. "We are relying on you, Josh. You need to put these pieces of the puzzle together for us and set out our case."

Josh gave a feeble smile. "He doesn't admit to anything specific. How will the court be able to find him guilty on any specific charges? We need more evidence. If you look at the time-stamp of the last recorded call, it was the evening before the search and seizure operation at his home, which explains why we managed to find all this evidence. Your timing was impeccable, he didn't even have time to destroy his files."

Detective Sidd and Josh sat staring out of the window at the city lights when they heard an email notification on Josh's computer. As if to answer Josh's prayer for more evidence he received an anonymous email from whistleblower_987@mail. com that stated:

Mr Carter,

I have information on the board members of Hillstrong Holdings that can assist you in your investigation.

If you are interested in pursuing everyone involved, meet me tomorrow at the Fine Dining restaurant in Mandela Square, Sandton City, at 12:00. The reservation will be under the name 'Ho'.

You may bring your investigating partner, but no one else. Whistleblower.

CHAPTER TWENTY-FOUR

Whistleblower

"**I** HAVE BEEN THINKING ABOUT that email we received last night. It's strange. On one hand it would make sense that there is huge public interest and so we are bound to find people who want to do the right thing, but the information that we need will have to come from someone on the inside, someone who was involved as well, and the consequences of being implicated are severe. We can probably expect someone asking for immunity to turn state witness, is my best guess," said Josh to Detective Sidd.

"I agree. We are going to have to play our hand very carefully today and see what this person has to say. I'll let you know as soon as I receive feedback from the IT technicians regarding tracking the IP address so that we can subpoena the email logs. Hopefully we get that before we meet with the Whistleblower."

"I have requested an expedited service on the process, so let's wait and see. I am interested to listen to more recordings while we have some time, before we go to Mandela Square," said Josh.

"Great. I have filled Rhonda in on the email and told her that we would update her immediately when we receive further information. She has other prosecutorial business to take care of today, but will be looking out for our call," said Detective Sidd as his phone rang. Once he saw who it was he answered immediately and motioned to Josh quietly. "I have to take this outside, you carry on without me," he mouthed, and left the boardroom.

Josh went through the list of call recordings dating further back. He would have to listen to each and every one of them. He listened through the calls and learned a few more details about Wikus Louw from the previous couple of months and discovered he was having an affair with a younger woman. Many of the calls that were recorded revealed evidence of an adulterous love affair between Wikus Louw and a young woman by the name of Mikayla. This, of course, had been published as a scandal in all the newspapers and on gossip sites. However, nothing seemed to be confirmed yet and much had been dismissed as rumours, until now.

The two lovers had made plans to travel the world together while Wikus attended his many business trips and he'd promised shopping sprees to spoil her while he conducted business. Mikayla had thanked Wikus for the extravagant gifts sent to her, such as a diamond necklace, gold wristwatch, and an imported coffee machine from Italy to remind her of the wonderful time they spent in an Italian coffee shop on one of their trips. It was clear that Wikus spared no expense on this woman to impress her – he had even bought her a luxury beach-front apartment in the Cape. And of course, a fancy sports car to go with it, a Bentley just like his, and, as he didn't want her to worry about parking that big car, a driver had come with it.

Detective Sidd stepped back into the boardroom briefly to tell Josh that something urgent had come up at the Commercial Crimes Office that he had to attend to.

"Is everything alright?" Josh asked when he saw an unpleasant expression on Detective Sidd's face.

"Yes, all fine, nothing to worry about. I'll meet you in Sandton at 12:00!" he said and left.

Josh continued to listen to more lovers' conversations. Some were made late at night while Wikus was working at home and his wife was sleeping in a nearby room. Then there were calls that involved business but did not contain enough context for Josh to clearly understand what transaction was taking place; it couldn't be easily proven that they were not legitimate.

The further back in time Josh went the less Wikus seemed to have used his office line for calls. Josh came to the last few calls on the server and one immediately caught his attention. Wikus was speaking to a well-educated Asian man with a heavy Chinese accent. Josh recognised the voice. Fei Hung and Wikus Louw were discussing the merger between Hung Industries and Hillstrong Holdings. Fei Hung was reporting to Wikus that he was unable to convince his board to go along with the transaction, the opposite of what he had told Josh, Detective Sidd and Rhonda when they'd had their video conference call.

He had told the three of them that he'd convinced his board not to conclude the transaction and that the board was basically placing pressure on him to proceed. Now Josh was hearing that Wikus and Fei Hung had, over a few calls, discussed the logistics of the merger and how their operations would be synergised for expansion across the Asian and African markets.

Had Fei Hung lied to them about his relationship with Wikus Louw? Wikus Louw ended the call by informing Fei Hung that they would have to proceed with their alternative business strategy now that their respective companies would not be merging and that each of them would have to make it convincing. What did that mean?

Josh looked at his watch: 11:20AM. He stood up and packed his things to go and meet the Whistleblower.

He arrived at Mandela Square and met up with Detective Sidd. Josh filled him in on everything that he had discovered on the calls.

"That doesn't make sense at all, though. What reason would Fei Hung have to lie to us about the situation? Surely he must know that we would find out the truth if we started investigating their relationship?" asked Detective Sidd.

"I don't know. That was my view as well. But if they continue to perform business together on side deals, naturally he would want to keep it quiet and throw us off."

At 11:55AM they entered the Fine Dining restaurant and told the maître' d' they were there to meet a friend and gave the reservation name. She directed them to the corner table where a gentleman sat alone, a man of Asian descent, smartly dressed in business attire, just like the rest of the Sandton population.

When they arrived at the table he did not stand up to greet them nor shake their hands but nodded at the maître'd'. "Thank you for coming, Mr Carter and Detective Sidd. Please sit, join me." They sat down and Josh looked around the restaurant casually to see whether anyone peculiar stood out as someone that may be watching the meet. "My name is Stan Ho and, as I have said, I have information that may be of interest to you in your investigation on Wikus Louw and Hillstrong Holdings. I realise that you may have some questions and so I shall hand over to you to ask them."

Josh took the lead on the meet. "Who are you and how do you have this information?"

"I am an intermediary acting for a friend from a large corporation who, at present, cannot risk letting his identity being known until you follow through with your investigation using the information that we have available for you," answered Stan Ho.

"Why is he assisting us? What does your source want in return?"

"Let's just say that both of your interests are aligned in ensuring that justice takes its course and the people involved are held responsible," said Stan Ho. He answered the questions carefully and methodically, without giving away any details.

"Where does the information come from and how was it obtained?" Josh asked.

"That is a little more difficult to explain. The information which I have with me, should you choose to accept it, has been collected from multiple sources which we identify for you in the dossier. We understand that certain of the documents were obtained, let's say, not by the usual channels. However, should you act in the correct way you will be able to procure the original documents for yourself in a way that allows your team to make use of them in the investigation and more particularly in the legal proceedings awaiting the guilty counterparts," he answered.

"When will we find out who your source is?" Josh asked.

"You will only find out his identity should you accept the information and charge the respective individuals with the crimes that they are guilty of. And even then, his identity must remain anonymous in your investigation reports."

"How do we know that we can trust you?" Josh asked rather foolishly, not expecting any answer of worth.

"You don't, Mr Carter. That will be completely up to you to decide upon. The information that we have procured is detailed enough to be able to verify and confirm the legitimacy thereof."

The risk Josh faced was accepting the information from a source that had in all likelihood obtained it illegally, or even fabricated it. This had multiple ramifications for them all. If the fact that it was obtained illegally ever got out, it could taint the whole investigation and render all their hard work futile as it would be thrown out of court before the trial had really begun. If there was one thing they couldn't risk it was not conducting the investigation in the most transparent manner possible. Everything had to be by the book on this one; there was too much at stake.

"It is a decision that I am sure you will need to consider together. I am going to go to the men's room and in the meantime the two of you can make your decision. I must be clear, if I leave this restaurant today without giving the information to you, I leave with the information and it will not become available to you again."

"We understand, thank you," said Josh. Stan Ho stood up and left the table and the moment he was out of earshot they started discussing the pros and cons of accepting the information.

"Let's assess the information that we have already. We can link Wikus Louw to many self-enriching deals that he concluded. He is the Chief Executive Officer of a public listed company where he did not conclude arms-length transactions. He had a personal financial interest in many of the deals for personal gain, and it looks like he has fudged the books and misrepresented the financial statements. At the moment, we cannot directly tie anyone else to the crimes that Wikus Louw will be charged with.

"We could possibly charge directors and business associates for being involved by association and see if we get lucky with poking enough holes in their testimony. However, it is unlikely that we would be able to, on that basis, prove beyond a reasonable doubt that anyone is guilty. When it comes to commercial crimes, the onus is extremely difficult. For directors to escape liability, they do not necessarily have to have made the correct decisions. They merely have to have acted reasonably in their duties and show that they did everything reasonably expected of a diligent director and made a decision on that basis."

"Shit, Josh, I just don't know," said Detective Sidd. "This information exchange could pay off and conclude the investigation with a smoking gun or, on the other hand, it could be a trap orchestrated by Wikus Louw himself that blows the investigation wide open."

"Let's call Rhonda. It is her investigation and she should make the call. My view is I think we should do it," said Josh. Josh called Rhonda but she was not available at that moment.

"Shit." Josh watched from across the room as Stan Ho was returning to the table.

Stan Ho sat down. "I understand that it is an important decision to make and I have not provided you with much time, but unfortunately I must be on my way. What will it be, Mr Carter?"

Detective Sidd looked uncertain, but Josh decided to go for it. "We will accept your information."

"Good," said Stan Ho and he nodded to someone on the other side of the restaurant. A large man, carrying a black leather briefcase, dressed in a suit and sunglasses, approached their table. He handed the briefcase to Stan Ho who in turn passed it to Josh. Josh stood up and took the briefcase from Stan Ho. The exchange was concluded.

"It was a pleasure to meet you both. Good luck with your investigation," said Stan Ho and stood up to leave.

"How do we get hold of you? Do we use the email account from last night?" asked Josh.

"No, that is unfortunately no longer secure. Once it is public knowledge that charges have been laid against the respective individuals, we will contact you," he said and walked out of the restaurant.

Josh and Detective Sidd sat back down at the table and not seconds later Rhonda Martins called. Perfect timing, thought Josh. He placed the call on speaker and updated her on the exchange.

"I hope your gut is correct, Josh. Review the evidence and report back as soon as you have something. Once we know what we are dealing with, we can have another briefing session at the Ranch House. The end of the year is approaching and we are running out of time; I would like to wrap it up before Christmas. Mark, please come through to the office."

"I'll work on it immediately and let you know," Josh said and ended the call.

Josh held the briefcase tightly. It had large brass buckles ensuring the safety of its contents. "I'm going to take this back to the office and start reviewing it so that we know what we are dealing with," he said.

Detective Sidd was reading a message on his phone and then said to Josh, "Great. I'll meet up with you later. Something I need to take care of. Let me know what the briefcase holds," he said, not giving any further explanation of his other matter.

Josh climbed into his BMW and made his way back to Carter & Associates. During the drive he found himself checking all of his mirrors repeatedly when stopping at a red light, making sure nobody could get close to the briefcase that was on his front passenger seat. He arrived at the office and asked Shirley to bring him some coffee and join him in the boardroom. Josh wanted a witness to opening the briefcase and would also need her to upload all of the documents onto the secure server to make them available to Rhonda and Detective Sidd remotely, after making a copy of all of the contents.

He opened the buckles of the briefcase. Inside was a thick beige dossier with labelled tabs with the names of five people. He recognised all of them. They were Hillstrong Holdings' Chief Executive Officer, Wikus Louw; Chief Financial Officer, Jacques Hendrik; founder and shareholder Karl Helmut; English businessman Winston Ainsley; and an Asian business man whose name Josh knew by more than just reference, Fei Hung of Hung Industries.

CHAPTER TWENTY-FIVE

Ranch House

JOSH ARRIVED AT THE GATES leading to the Ranch House for the last briefing session of the year. He was alone this time; Gabby and Daniel were arranging the movers for the new house. There would be two moving trucks in the same street, one for Josh's house and the other would park across the road at Gabby's, but both trucks would go to the same location. Gabby had already taken stock of both sets of furniture and knew where they would be best suited in the new house. They would also need more furniture to fill up the big house, of course, which excited her and made Josh nervous.

Josh parked his BMW outside of the gates of the Ranch House, went through the usual security search routine and proceeded to the main building. Detective Sidd's police cruiser was there already, parked next to Rhonda's SUV. He walked to the large double doors, greeted the massive security guards and entered the Ranch House. There were Christmas decorations hanging from the rafters and a Christmas tree by the large window overlooking the Mkuze River. Detective Sidd and Rhonda were deep in hushed conversation when Josh approached the room. He could barely make out what they were talking about.

Rhonda Martins asked, "Are you sure? Do you have enough evidence to proceed with the arrest?"

Detective Sidd answered her, "Yes. It saddens me to say that we have everything we need and the evidence is conclusive."

"How will we tell him? He is going to be shattered by the news," said Rhonda.

As Josh entered the room they stopped talking immediately. Josh thought it was strange that they did this. They knew they would be able to trust his confidentiality on all matters, irrespective of whether it was an investigation that he was involved in or not. Unless, they were talking about him.

"Josh, how are you?" asked Rhonda.

"Well, thanks. I'm eager to get this investigation wrapped up before the end of the year, I think we are just about ready," he said.

The three of them sat at the large conference room table and discussed the contents of the dossier and the five people that were named.

Josh started with the evidence of their main accused. "Wikus Louw, just as we concluded by reviewing the files in his home office, has been benefiting financially from side deals prior to large transactions with Hillstrong Holdings. The amounts run into the hundreds of millions per transaction. He has accumulated approximately R3.5 billion, according to the evidence we have already reviewed.

"Tied into the same transactions are the other four men that we have information on. Jacques Hendrik, Chief Financial Officer of the Hillstrong Group, including its international arms, has been doing the financials for most of the transactions. However, it seems he does not benefit from any shareholding like the others. Instead, he receives large bonuses for the successful completion of the deals.

"It remains unclear whether he has actual knowledge of the illegal dealings, although it is highly irregular that a person in his position would not raise important questions that are necessary for completing the financials for the year. This in itself is enough to charge and question him on his position and role in the company.

"There are multiple investment companies that have performed many transactions with the Hillstrong Group, all of which have not been disclosed in the financial statements nor recorded in the minutes of directors and shareholders meetings. These companies are the companies of Winston Ainsley, one of Wikus' business partners. Wikus has an interest in these companies in the United Kingdom and certain European companies as well and receives dividends as a shareholder after the successful transactions.

"Coming back to the South African structure, as well as the branches in Germany, Karl Helmut, founder and shareholder of Hillstrong Holdings, has a family trust that has been receiving billions along with Wikus' family trust. Although his signature is not on any of the written agreements that were concluded, he has been receiving financial benefits as a result of the illegal transactions.

"Included in this self-enriching scheme is the last person in our dossier, Fei Hung. This was the odd name out when we received the dossier, until I realised that we had collected evidence on him earlier. FH Incorporated, the special purpose vehicle that has the corporate lawyer director on the board who is protected by attorney-client privilege, stands for Fei Hung Incorporated.

"Mr Hung lied to us during our video conference here at the Ranch House. He told us that the board put pressure on him to conclude the merger with Hillstrong Holdings and he was able to persuade them otherwise. Well, some digging has provided information that it was the other way around. He put forward the proposal to the board that rejected his plea to deal with

Hillstrong Holdings." Josh finished the summary of his part of the investigation.

Rhonda took over. "We have great relationships with both the United Kingdom and Chinese authorities. I will share our information with them to conclude a co-ordinated action. When we arrest and press charges on Wikus, Jacques Hendrik here in South Africa, and hopefully Karl Helmut, unless he is in Germany, in which case we will speak to the German authorities, Winston Ainsley and Fei Hung will be apprehended too and charged in their jurisdictions."

Detective Sidd asked the question that was still bothering him. "The condition that was given for receiving the identity of the source of the information was that the persons mentioned in the dossier were to be arrested and charged. In order for that to happen, there would need to be evidence of the crimes being committed. Do I proceed with the arrests based on the information at hand without knowing the source?"

Josh answered. "This is the predicament that we as the investigative team finds ourselves in. We have the evidence, but it was included in the dossier and not collected first hand. The Public Prosecutor's Office will not be able to assert that the evidence was not improperly obtained, until the source verifies how the evidence came to be collected. Lawyers for the accused will immediately apply to court to have the evidence excluded for reasons of inadmissibility based on the fact that it was unlawfully obtained, if that was indeed the case.

"On the one hand, we do not want to show our hand and make the arrests before knowing the source, but we are also heavily relying on the information in the dossier. It is our only play at the moment. From a legal standpoint, it is possible that the evidence be conditionally admissible for the trial. This means that evidence can be admitted on condition that some defect which renders it inadmissible is cured during the course of the trial. The procedure is rare and only followed in certain circumstances. I am confident that I can work with Rhonda and set out a case for this!"

"As much as I want these guys to be locked up, I'm not sure I'm comfortable with making these arrests without being sure. I also don't want my family to become a target," said Detective Sidd.

"I appreciate that, Mark. That is exactly what I have been going through with Gabby and Daniel. We have had security around for months now and we have had to put up with it," answered Josh, slightly annoyed that he had put so much effort into this case only to experience flaky nerves from his team members. He was also annoyed about Rhonda and Detective Sidd having had a conversation that he assumed was about himself.

Rhonda intervened to prevent internal tension. "Mark, why don't I talk you through the evidence after our meeting to give you comfort and show you the matters I have handled in the past," she said.

They had found some damning evidence and were feeling hopeful for the first time in this case. The only concern was whether the documents were legitimate and not fraudulent and how many of the documents in the dossier were actually lawfully obtained. If they were not, the question was whether the documents could subsequently be lawfully obtained by the team. It was a huge risk to consider. It would either pay off and they would make history, or they would get it horribly wrong and also make history, but for all the wrong reasons.

"Mark, tell us your feedback from tracking down the company hired to move Hillstrong's documents off-site."

"The movers, Corporate Storage, were paid an exorbitant fee for the removal of three truckloads of documents to a storage facility. They were also instructed to destroy ten boxes of documents, which they did at an abandoned warehouse. The boxes of documents were incinerated, never to be seen again.

"The movers were reluctant to provide any information at first, but once I advised them they had committed the crimes of obstruction of justice and acting as an accomplice for one of the biggest fraud cases that South Africa has ever seen and that a prison sentence was on the table, they were cooperative and told me exactly where the rest of the documents were. The documents that were not destroyed were standard, legitimate documents and company policies that were of no help to us."

"My guess is that they were trying to use the off-site storage of the documents as an excuse for certain documents to go missing and possibly blame the moving company when they could not produce documents that would be subpoenaed," said Josh, regaining his calm after showing his annoyance towards Detective Sidd.

"Alright, that's the evidence we have so far. Mark, after we go through everything, once you're comfortable, I will have the arrest warrants approved. You get your teams briefed and in place for the arrests to take place tomorrow afternoon."

***

Josh arrived home, at his new house. He pulled his BMW into the driveway and parked it next to Gabby's car and his Ducati Motorcycle in the triple garage. He entered the house and found Gabby and Daniel unpacking the last of the boxes. The furniture was all where it was supposed to be, as Gabby explained, and the clothes were all packed away. Gabby was excited to show Josh that she had done up his office for him.

Josh walked into his newly furnished office, with brand new bookshelves covering the walls, a matching dark cherry wood desk, and a luxury leather office chair. He looked at Gabby, battling to find the words. "This is incredible Gabs, how did you…?" was all he managed to get out. He had forgotten all about his bad mood with the investigation.

She smiled at him, so thankful that he liked his surprise.

"Your Christmas present from Daniel and me. We want to thank you for everything you have done for us," she said.

"I love it, thank you!" he said as he pulled her closer and kissed her. They stood and admired the room for a while. His books were packed on the shelves, all in the exact same places as before, and now the office was everything he'd dreamed of for his home. The large window gave a perfect view of the yard where he would create his Japanese garden. The pond was already there and the water, tested for his koi which had been quarantined for the past two days, was slowly being mixed into the drums of water where the fish were kept before being put into their new home. The rest of the garden would be completed in stages: the miniature river and bridge across it, the layers of rocks and Japanese plants comprising of bonsais and a small cherry blossom tree, and many other features.

The doorbell rang. "Oh, that's for me," said Gabby. "I ordered pizza. I didn't feel like cooking after all the unpacking. I bought wine as well. I have already set up some plates outside by the pool." She ran down the stairs to the front door.

Josh sat in his leather chair. The leather squeaked as he sat down. Such comfort. He could smell the new leather smell. He breathed it in and slowly exhaled. It gave him an accomplished feeling. It smelt just as good as a new car smell.

He thought about the year that had passed and the investigation that was about to come to a close. Of course, in the same breath it could be said that it was just the beginning because the investigation would go to trial and, although he wouldn't be appearing in court, he would be consulting with Rhonda and Detective Sidd for the duration of it.

His thoughts then turned to his parents. He had still not made much headway with the claim for their retirement funds. The paperwork in respect of deceased estates was always a slow, drawn-out process, especially with a person who dies intestate, meaning without a final Will and Testament. He had phoned his father during the drive home from the Ranch House and his father had told him that he had sold the race car. This upset Josh more than he wanted to think about. It made him angry. He breathed in the leather smell again and exhaled slowly.

"Josh! Please come downstairs," he heard Gabby shout. He made his way to the kitchen where he found Detective Sidd waiting for him. Gabby started to leave, but Detective Sidd stopped her.

"Wait, I need to talk to the both of you," he said, in a serious tone.

"What's wrong, Mark?" asked Josh.

"We have discovered who poisoned you. We made the arrest a short while ago," he said.

"But that's great!" said Josh, confused as to why Detective Sidd wasn't sharing his enthusiasm. "What aren't you telling us?" he asked further.

"You were not the target. It appears that it was meant for Gabby. Only one of the glasses that you guys drank from contained traces of the poison and Gabby was supposed to drink it," said Detective Sidd.

Josh and Gabby were shocked. "How do you know that? Who was behind it?" asked Josh. Detective Sidd was battling to find the words. "Mark! Who?" demanded Josh.

"It was Vivian Rose," he said.

Josh felt sick. "Vee? Are you sure? No, I don't believe it. Surely not, why would she do that? You guys must have made a mistake."

Gabby burst out crying and Josh held her close as she sobbed.

"She is being interrogated as we speak, but from the comments she made during her arrest it appears she was trying to get Gabby out of the picture and bond with you over the loss of a loved one, the way that she bonded with you when her husband died," said Detective Sidd.

"But what about at the hospital, the guys from the gym? Those two men tried to kill me. Was that her as well?" Josh asked.

"Well, you see, that is the confusing part. That does not seem to be related at all. It was someone feeling opportunistic who tried to take advantage of the situation, make it look like finishing the same job. We have subpoenaed the log records and personal details of the members at the gym and we will obtain their information and make that arrest as well.

"I can't imagine how difficult it must be to hear this news, for both of you. I'm sorry for coming by and shocking you with it; I just wanted to do this in person," he added.

"How long have you known about this?" asked Josh.

Detective Sidd looked ashamed. "For a while now. Rhonda and I didn't want to say anything unless we were sure. I'm sorry, Josh."

Josh said nothing. This explained why Detective Sidd had been acting strangely for the past few weeks.

Detective Sidd left Josh and Gabby in the kitchen. Josh felt betrayed and upset for Gabby's sake. She didn't deserve this.

"Gabs, I'm so sorry, I don't even know what to say!" he said.

"Don't apologise, it's not your fault, how could you have known? She obviously needs help, and I was starting to really like her!" said Gabby, wiping away her tears.

CHAPTER TWENTY-SIX

Arrested and Charged

IT WAS ON A FRIDAY evening two days before Christmas that the public prosecutor approved the warrant for the arrest of Wikus Louw, Jacques Hendrik and Karl Helmut, in South Africa. The UK Commercial Crimes Unit, working in collaboration with the South African arm, issued the arrest warrant for Winston Ainsley and the Chinese government, were staking out Hung Industries to capture and arrest Fei Hung. Detective Sidd and Rhonda would be making history at this very moment.

"I wonder how everything is going down," Josh said to Gabby, thinking about arresting Wikus Louw.

"Didn't you want to go along?" she asked.

"No, they offered but I declined. I have played my part and now it's time to leave the rest up to them. Besides, I wanted to just spend the time with you," he said. "Mark said he would let me know how it went as soon as it's over, anyway."

Josh and Gabby were sitting on their new outdoor furniture set on their bedroom balcony staring out at the city of Johannesburg, drinking a glass of wine. They were enjoying the December air and taking a quiet moment together to relax. Daniel was sleeping already, exhausted from playing in the pool and riding his bicycle around all day. The small garden lanterns glowed in the dark, illuminating the Japanese garden that was starting to take form. The city lights could be seen in the distance along the quiet streets of Sandton. Josh wondered what it was going to be like for the Hillstrong Holdings executives, about to find out that their Christmas would be spent behind bars. In contrast, he was going to have his first real vacation in a long time.

"I'm looking forward to going to the beach," he said.

"Me too. It's been so long since I've been there: sun, sea and surf. It's going to be amazing together, the three of us," she said, looking very relaxed. The wine had probably helped a lot with that. The shock of the news that Vivian had tried to kill her had subsided, but Josh could see that the last twelve months had taken a toll on her either way. All they had left for the rest of the year was to enjoy the Christmas season.

It was just before 11PM when Josh's phone lit up with a message from Detective Sidd: "Operation Steinopoly was a success" it read. Josh read it to Gabby. It was he who'd come up with the name of the stealth operation. He made up the word by using "Stein", meaning stone in German – the first piece of furniture that Hillstrong created had had legs of stone – and 'opoly' shortened from the word monopoly, which was what the Hillstrong group of companies had set out to do; to take their first created piece of furniture that gave them a name for themselves and create a monopoly in the furniture market; to have the exclusive possession and control of the supply chain and trade its products throughout the world. Their goal was to become the largest furniture manufacturer and retailer in the world, to be even greater than Ikea. Josh, satisfied that his hard work had paid off, could now retire to bed for the night.

***

Josh woke on Saturday morning, left his room and walked downstairs to the kitchen and switched on the TV on the kitchen island to hear the news reports flooding in on every channel.

Breaking News: Hillstrong Holdings' executives arrested and charged with money laundering, corporate fraud and illegally benefiting from the transactions of public listed companies.

Sources say late last night, three special ops teams stationed themselves outside the residences of ex-Chief Executive Officer Wikus Louw, Chief Financial Officer Jacques Hendrik and founder and largest shareholder of Hillstrong Holdings, Karl Helmut, and arrested the three businessmen for causing the largest corporate crash the South African stock market has ever experienced.

Stay tuned to follow the live updates of the arrests of Hillstrong's top brass.

It was finally done, the risk had been taken and now what would be, would be. He poured a cup of coffee freshly brewed by the percolator and walked back upstairs. Gabby was still sleeping; the sun was barely up. He decided to put on his running shoes and take a jog. He left a note next to Gabby's bedside and left the house. The roads were quiet; the new neighbourhood was still sleeping. He would have to find a new jogging route now. The immediate vicinity consisted of hills that would make for great strength training.

He ran on the outskirts of the hills above Sandton, enjoying the views of the jacaranda trees and high rises in the distance. He stopped under a tree out of the morning sun and looked out at the city; he could see the offices of Carter & Associates from where he stood. He decided he would go see what the place looked like, now that all the servers and filing cabinets had been removed. He ran past Isabelle's. The place was dead, closed down since Vee had been arrested with FOR SALE signs over the glass windows. It would usually have been open and the staff would have been there cleaning and setting up the tables for the Christmas lunch goers and the chef would have specials for the Christmas period, usually a buffet.

Josh still could not believe that Vee would have gone to those lengths. He thought back to all the late nights and dinners they'd had together; she'd never truly told him how she felt. He assumed the nights they spent together were just comfort for the loneliness they both sometimes felt. Then he thought about all the times he'd spoken to her about Gabby and the times that she'd encouraged him to make a move and ask her out. He felt sick just thinking about it. Was that all part of her plan? To make him fall in love with Gabby only to take her away from him so that she could be there for him when he grieved?

He didn't want to think about it anymore and continued to jog. He arrived at his office, typed in the pin to the magnetic locking system and gained access to Carter & Associates. The War Room had become a normal legal office boardroom again. There were no papers on the tables and floors, the white boards were cleaned and the photographs had been taken down. The filing cabinets were gone and the office was neat and tidy.

He went into his office and found a couple of envelopes on his desk that Shirley had placed there for him. He picked them up, left the office and started the jog back home. The way back was much tougher, being uphill most of the way. A few days like this a week and he would be in peak performance in no time.

He walked the last few hundred metres to his home and found Gabby in the kitchen making breakfast, also watching the news. He kissed her on the forehead.

"You're all sweaty!" she played.

"I forgot how many hills were around here. It's going to take some getting used to," he said and threw the letters from his office on the kitchen counter.

"Did we already get mail at our new home?" she asked in disbelief.

"No, I jogged past the office, Shirley must have left them for me, knowing that I would be back there before the new year," he said.

"You ran all the way to the office? No wonder you're so sweaty!" she said. "Go take a shower quick and breakfast will be ready when you get back."

Josh walked back upstairs to take a shower as the news in the kitchen continued with the story.

> *In a night operation called Operation Steinopoly, three executives of Hillstrong Holdings were arrested for the corporate crash that has shocked the nation...*

Josh smiled to himself. Detective Sidd must have leaked the name of the operation to the news reporters.

> *...we have just received word that two other international businessmen have also been arrested in connection with the crimes committed on the stock exchanges in respect of Hillstrong Holdings. These men are Chief Executive Officer and Founder of Hung Industries, Fei Hung in Hong Kong, China, and infamous English businessman and real estate tycoon Winston Ainsley, in the United Kingdom...*

Josh showered and went back downstairs to enjoy a breakfast of waffles, eggs and bacon. Daniel was having waffles and syrup and so was Gabby. They discussed their beach holiday, arranged for after Christmas. Daniel couldn't wait to pack his suitcase.

Josh told him that they were taking the BMW so he had to pack light, which was fine with Daniel. Gabby had a house to show last minute for a client on Christmas Eve; someone wanted to surprise their significant other for Christmas. She had also promised to take Daniel to her parents for a visit. Josh had something to take care of as well.

After breakfast, Josh climbed into his car and phoned his father and asked him to meet him at a local car garage that they used to go to often when he was younger. Josh arrived ten minutes early and met Darryl, the shop owner and mechanic. He was an elderly but stockily-built man in greasy overalls and steel capped shoes, about Josh's father's age.

"Hey, Uncle D! Merry Christmas," said Josh.

"Joshy boy! Same to you! Congrats on your big investigation, I'm so glad you nailed those bastards!" said Darryl.

"Well, it's not over yet. Trial is a whole other story, but we will get them. Is everything ready?" he asked.

"Yip, just as you asked, Joshy boy. It's over there in the corner under that cover. Just finished polishing it this morning so it looks great. It has new tyres, brake pads, and cone filter – the whole works!" he said, extremely proud of what he had accomplished.

"Thanks, Uncle D!" said Josh as his father arrive outside.

Alan Carter entered the garage. "Hi Darryl, Josh! What are you boys up to on the day before Christmas?" he asked.

"Hi Dad." Josh hugged his father in a tight embrace. Darryl and Alan Carter shook hands. They were well acquainted after years of working together on cars, and sharing the same racing circles.

"We have something to show you, Alan," said Darryl.

"Oh yeah, what's that?" asked Alan.

"It's over there in the corner. Let's go take a look," said Josh. "Uncle D, would you mind pulling the covers?"

"With pleasure!" said Darryl. He stood behind the covered car, gripped a handful of the car polyester cover and yanked the covers hard to expose the car beneath it.

"Wow!" said Alan looking at the bright orange, BMW M3 race car with full slick tyres. "She's a beaut! What's under the hood?" he added.

"3.2 litre M3 motor with full race spec exhaust system," said Josh.

"I bet she purrs like a dream," said Alan.

Darryl opened the door to the race car, placed each leg over the roll cage and looked up at Josh, who nodded at him. Darryl turned the ignition. Immediately the roar of the engine filled the garage. Darryl waited a minute or two to warm up the engine and revved it gently at first and then made it roar.

Alan's eyes were alive with passion for the machine – he lived for cars, engines, any fast machines. Alan walked around the car, stopping to inspect and admire the body work, the racing brakes. He climbed into the passenger side of the car and ran his hand over the smooth carbon fibre dash that was created for weight reduction and which contained rocket-ship-looking switches, all neatly finished, the way that Alan would approve of.

Darryl switched off the car and the two of them climbed out.

"Wow, boy, its great! It's an absolute beast. I can't imagine what it would do on the track!" said Alan.

Josh knew that his father had always wanted a 3.2 litre M3 race car, but it had been just out of reach financially. Retirement was more important and now that his retirement savings were almost all lost it was a distant dream.

"Who did you build it for, Darryl? Has he joined the BMW Race Series for next year?" Alan asked. It would definitely be a race car that he looked out for from the grandstands. Darryl said nothing but waited for Josh to jump in.

"It's yours, Dad," Josh said.

"You're kidding! What do you mean?" asked Alan, in disbelief.

"I had it built for you," said his son. "Merry Christmas."

"No, boy, how could you do this? It must have cost a fortune," he said. "Are you serious?" he asked again.

"I got a big bonus for the Hillstrong investigation and you sold your race car because of losing your retirement funds. You always wanted an M3," Josh said.

Alan's eyes welled up. A giant man, brought to his knees. It had been an incredibly stressful year for him.

Josh embraced his father. "I love you, Dad!"

"I love you too, my boy," he said. "I don't have the words."

"I know. Let's take it for a spin, what do you say?"

"Definitely," said Alan and he wasted no time in climbing into the driver's side of the polished orange race car. Darryl opened the double glass doors of the garage onto the street. Alan Carter ignited the engine and made it roar. He slowly edged out of the garage and breathed in deeply as he squeezed the steering wheel. Josh, as if he were a young boy, looked at his father, who gazed back at him, gave him a wink and pressed his right foot flat, bringing the power of the BMW from the front engine to the rear tyres. The screech could be heard around the block.

They raced around the neighbourhood together, the way they would when Josh was younger, and afterwards quickly parked the car in the garage before the police showed up. Darryl had a bakkie and a trailer ready to deliver the car to Alan's house.

"I have to go back home to pack for my holiday with Gabby and Daniel. I'll see you at the house later for Christmas dinner, Dad," he said. He wished Darryl Merry Christmas again and thanked him for all his hard work. He couldn't remember when last he had seen his father so happy.

CHAPTER TWENTY-SEVEN

Christmas

CHRISTMAS EVE DINNER COULD BE smelt from Josh and Gabby's new kitchen. The spinach and feta stuffed duck had just been taken out of the oven as Josh's parents arrived. Josh and Gabby's bags were packed and ready by the front door. The plan was to open presents with the family that night, and take a slow drive down to the beach on Christmas morning, while the roads were quiet.

Everyone was in a great mood. Christmas music was playing, compliments of Michael Bublé, through the stereo. Josh's mother was sitting on the lounge carpet talking to Daniel as he showed her his new toys that Santa Claus had given him.

Josh had just received word from the estates lawyer handling Nicholas Nel's affairs that the investors whose money had been fraudulently invested in Hillstrong would receive ninety percent of their investments back from the estate, thanks to the voice recorded settlement agreement in the interrogation room at Randburg Station. The remaining millions were going to his ex-wife and child to whom he'd never paid any child support. It was the best outcome anyone could have hoped for. Josh's parents were now stress free; a huge weight had been lifted off their shoulders.

Daniel opened his present from Josh. It was the drone he had been eyeing for months in Hamley's toy shop.

"We can fly it on the beach soon, I promise," Josh said.

"You spoiled him, again," said Gabby and then she kissed Josh and put her arm around his waist. "I love all of my gifts too!" she said referring to the diamond tennis bracelet, black and pink Nike running shoes and an IPod to match.

"There is one more present on the tree that hasn't been opened yet," said Josh as he walked over to the tree and picked up a Christmas decoration that had been hanging there for the past few weeks. It was a miniature gingerbread house covered with gumdrops, candy-canes, Christmas decorations, and snow enclosed in a snow globe. He handed it to Gabby who said thanks and laughed as if he were making a joke by buying it for her. She stared at it, not fully understanding what she was supposed to do with it.

"What is it, exactly?" she asked.

"Open it, from the front. There is a small clasp at the base of the globe," he said.

She hadn't even seen the clasp with all the detail around the base, she flipped it up and pulled the top part away from the bottom, exposing a black suede cushion holding a large diamond ring. She lost her breath and put her hands up to her mouth. Josh's mother cried out with joy and his father cheered. Gabby was quiet as Josh moved closer to her, now on one knee. Her eyes immediately filled up with tears.

"Gabriela Riley, the last year has been one incredible journey and it made me realise that it doesn't matter what life throws at you, as long as you have someone amazing at your side. I want this life to continue forever, with you and Daniel. Will you make me the happiest man alive, and be my wife?"

"Oh Josh! Yes, of course I will!"

The whole family cheered, especially Daniel. They brought out the champagne and celebrated Christmas Eve with the clinking of glasses.

CHAPTER TWENTY-EIGHT

Letter

Wikus Louw, Jacques Hendrik and Karl Helmut were all in private accommodation, but not the luxury type that they were used to. The floors were hard, cold concrete with stains. There was a small window in each of their rooms with thick reinforced steel bars and an en-suite bathroom – actually an open plan bathroom and bedroom all in one, which smelled terrible. The toilets were missing their seats and covers and the bars to their cells were greasy from the hands of the many accused who had passed through the awaiting trial prisoner cells. The stench was worse than any racing horse stable that Wikus Louw had ever experienced. He constantly wanted to gag. The food was a mush meal of who knows what, he wouldn't even feed it to the pigs on his farm.

His Christmas was going to be a long and drawn out one. The courts would open in the New Year, where he would have to plead guilty or not guilty and request bail, which would more than likely be denied. It was unlikely that the prosecution would even consider a plea settlement. The community would never allow that; they wanted blood.

Wikus Louw's loyal associate Willem had been arrested for conspiracy to commit murder by instructing two men, Dale Roberts and Earl Phillips, to murder Josh in the hospital. Dale and Earl were on the run.

The whistle-blower had revealed himself; it was Simon Chen, Fei Hung's personal advisor and assistant. He had been collecting information on his ex-boss's illegal dealings for years. He had been offered a promotion and a large raise under the new leadership of Hung Industries, now that the ex-chairman and ex-CEO was no longer affiliated with the group of companies. He had informed the investigation team where to find all of the information that he had included in the dossier first hand. He would be testifying under witness protection and *in camera*. The Public Prosecutor's Office was ready to proceed with the trial.

***

Josh, Gabby and Daniel drove along the coastline in Josh's BMW convertible with the roof down. Summer music played from the speakers. Gabby's hair blew in the wind and Daniel played with a toy aeroplane on the back seat. Life was perfect. Gabby kept admiring her left hand with the diamond sparkling in the sun. She held Josh's hand with her other while they drove. The year had been long, but worth it.

"What was that letter about, the one you were reading in the kitchen this morning?" she asked.

"A new investigation," he replied.

"Another one? I hope it's not like the last one."

"I will be meeting someone in the New Year and then I'll find out about the details," he said. He recited the handwritten letter in his head.

Mr Carter,

There is an anonymous group called by many names, one of which is "The Hackers", who are threatening to breach high security data servers. The aim is to gain leverage over high government officials and political advisors as far up as the presidential cabinet.

The list of targets for this interception and data breach comprise some of the largest corporations, holding data of people all over the world. Billions of records consisting of personal information, financial and employment, the consequences could bring a collapse to the economy of the country and threaten our trading arrangements with many countries.

The internet connects the entire world online; the amount of data that is exchanged is enormous. The amount of personal information and data at risk would put WikiLeaks and the Panama Papers to shame. The consequences would be catastrophic! For this reason we have contacted you via post, we will have to go back in time to fight against these futuristic criminals.

We request a meet in the New Year to offer you a position in the investigation team.

We will get hold of you closer to the time to discuss arrangements.

Josh already knew he would accept the assignment. Once the Hillstrong trial was under way, he would need to focus on his own firm again. It was clear that he was making a name for himself in the investigative world of law and business.

Wikus Louw briefly crossed his mind. He thought of the artwork in the Louw Mansion. One piece in particular made him remember a quote he had once read. It was the oil on canvas painting of Napoleon Crossing the Alps. The quote was *"Great ambition is the passion of a great character. Those endowed with it may perform very good or very bad acts. All depends on the principle which direct them."*

Josh considered himself a man of great ambition and that he would decide each day to live a life of good principles.